He was standing so close, his finger was practically the only thing between their lips.

She was very tempted to push it out of the way. Instead, she took a step even further over that line.

"It's all I need." She held eye contact with him, saw the darkening of his pupils, the tick in his jaw as he clenched his teeth together. There was a power in knowing, seeing, that she affected him just as much as he did her.

Her gaze fell to his mouth. She wanted to feel his lips hard and insistent on hers, his beard grazing her skin, turning her insides to mush in the process. It was nice to feel something other than fear being this close to a man again. Even if it still represented a danger of sorts. Though, in that moment, she didn't care about the repercussions of straying beyond the boundaries of their working relationship. All that mattered was the notion that he was about to kiss her.

Dear Reader,

One of the great things about being a writer is the "research" we do before we put pen to paper. Every experience usually finds its way into a book at some point. So, when I had the pleasure of taking part in a chocolate-making class, I knew someday I'd be writing about a chocolatier. Cue my feisty, courageous heroine, Bonnie Abernathy!

And where better to open a chocolate shop than in a castle. A good excuse to go exploring Scottish castles, and the perfect opportunity to introduce a handsome kilted duke to go with it.

Ewen Harris is reluctant to let Bonnie into his life, but she leaves him no choice. Both wounded by the past and full of fears about the future, they soon come to rely on one another. Something that terrifies them both.

It's an emotional journey, best enjoyed with some chocolate at hand!

Happy reading.

Karin xx

Highland Fling
with Her Boss

———

Karin Baine

Recycling programs
for this product may
not exist in your area.

ISBN-13: 978-1-335-59665-9

Highland Fling with Her Boss

Harlequin Enterprises ULC
22 Adelaide St. West, 41st Floor
Toronto, Ontario M5H 4E3, Canada
www.Harlequin.com

Printed in U.S.A.

Karin Baine lives in Northern Ireland with her husband, two sons and her out-of-control notebook collection. Her mother and her grandmother's vast collection of books inspired her love of reading and her dream of becoming a Harlequin author. Now she can tell people she has a *proper* job! You can follow Karin on Twitter @karinbaine1 or visit her website for the latest news, karinbaine.com.

Books by Karin Baine

Harlequin Romance

Pregnant Princess at the Altar

Harlequin Medical Romance

Carey Cove Midwives

Festive Fling to Forever

Royal Docs

Surgeon Prince's Fake Fiancée
A Mother for His Little Princess

Wed for Their One Night Baby
A GP to Steal His Heart
Single Dad for the Heart Doctor
Falling Again for the Surgeon
Nurse's Risk with the Rebel
An American Doctor in Ireland

Visit the Author Profile page
at Harlequin.com for more titles.

For anyone who needs to hear it—You are enough xx

CHAPTER ONE

BONNIE COULD ALMOST hear the carriage wheels trundling over the stone bridge, the clip-clop of horses' hooves, maybe even a piper at the entrance of the castle to welcome visitors. BenCrag Castle certainly didn't look as if it had changed in the three hundred years it had stood proudly on the Scottish Ayrshire cliffs, yet she trusted it had been modernised inside. Otherwise the chocolate shop she was about to open in it was going to look very out of place.

'You'd think they'd have sent someone to meet me,' she muttered to herself. What she wouldn't do now for a horse and carriage, or even a lift on the back of a tractor.

It had been a long walk from the bus stop, down through the trees, sun blazing, carrying all of her worldly possessions. Not that she had much to call her own. Ed had paid for everything during their relationship, that was how he'd wooed her, by treating her like a queen and lavishing her with gifts. To an only child, who'd been wrapped in cotton wool by her parents, it had been exciting to have Ed pursue her, taking her places she'd never been before. They'd dined in fancy restaurants, gone on exotic holidays, and he'd bought her new clothes to go with her exciting new life. The family home and chocolate shop her entire world up until then.

Looking back, she'd been naïve. Probably because she'd been so protected from the world. Ed had seemed like the handsome prince in her childish fairy tales come to life, whisking her away from a life of drudgery working in her father's chocolate shop to a happy ever after with the love of her life. He couldn't do enough to make her happy and she'd felt like the luckiest girl in the world. It had been an easy decision to move out of her home and go to live with him, even if it had caused a rift between her and her family.

She'd discovered too late that Ed thought she was just another one of his possessions. Before long, he'd isolated her from the few friends she'd had, and begun criticising her appearance and questioning her every move, until she'd barely left the house. Cut off from everyone, she'd thought she had no choice but to remain in the relationship, until he'd started pushing her for a family, and she'd known she couldn't subject a child to the same treatment. Then he'd raised his fists…

Bonnie shivered, despite the heat. It had taken some planning to make her escape, saving the little money she had and reaching out to a domestic abuse charity, who'd eventually convinced her to press charges and found her a refuge to stay in. That was when she'd seen the ad for the café in the castle and persuaded the duke she could go one better with a chocolate shop, finally putting the skills she'd learned in the family business to good use.

She'd even managed to convince him to let her live on site, giving her the impression he was quite lonely up here in his castle. A castle! Bonnie couldn't believe this was going to be her new home for the foreseeable future. After the nightmare she'd been living for too long, it seemed like a fairy tale. She just wished she'd been able to get hold of him before she'd made the journey. It had been weeks since he'd answered any of her calls or messages, but she supposed he was busy with the summer season coming up, and she had a contract. There was no backing out now.

Trailing her trolley suitcase behind her, she took a deep breath and crossed through the archway into the courtyard, marvelling at the turrets and ramparts towering above her. She marched up to the large oak door with iron hinges and studding, and lifted the lion-shaped knocker, the sound of which seemed to reverberate through the whole building when she let it fall again.

Bonnie straightened herself up, tried to flatten her wayward chestnut curtain of hair, and waited to face her new employer. And waited. She knocked again. By the third attempt she was beginning to lose patience, wondering what kind of set-up she'd got herself into if they didn't even have enough staff to open the door. It didn't bode well for getting customers into her new chocolate shop.

The sound of clipped footsteps on hard flooring sounded behind the door, marking someone's journey to meet her. Then a scowling man yanked the door open and barked a 'What?' at her.

'I, er, I'm looking for the duke,' she stuttered, thrown by the hostile reception.

'We're closed,' he spat, and slammed the door shut, the din scaring the birds from the neighbouring tree tops.

Bonnie took a step back, startled by the brief, brutal interaction. Although these months on her own had been building her confidence again, she still found a domineering man triggering. The scars from her relationship with Ed were still raw. Even though she'd had counselling at the refuge and Ed was currently serving four years in prison, it was difficult to get past those wounds. Though, deep down, she knew now that she wasn't to blame for what had happened, that he'd manipulated her and abused her trust, she naturally remained wary of other men. More aware of the need to protect herself.

Tempted though she was to slink away again, she had nowhere else to go. Besides, as another member of staff, she had as much right as the grumpy butler to be here.

She knocked again. When there was no forthcoming answer, despite her presence having been acknowledged in some capacity, she decided to try and find another way inside.

Of course, the duke wouldn't open his front door himself, but she was sure he was in residence and would be able to clear up any confusion over her arrival. All she had to do was bypass the surly gatekeeper standing in the way of her new life.

With renewed purpose she turned and made her way around the side of the castle, looking for the back door. There was always a secret tradesman's entrance in these places, so the lowly staff didn't sully the eyeballs of the well-heeled residents by being seen. Although she got the impression times had moved on and the duke was much more accommodating, her presence had already apparently upset someone.

However, her new nemesis was interfering with her plan b, gathering some freshly cut logs from the woodpile near the back door. He rolled his eyes and tutted when he saw her approach. Bonnie swallowed down the rise of bile in her throat, and braced herself for the confrontation she knew she had to have if she was going to get her new start.

'I need to see the duke. He's expecting me.'

'Oh?' Now that he'd stopped frowning, raising an eyebrow only, she could see he was quite handsome in that outdoorsy, farmhand kind of way.

She noted that he wasn't actually wearing any sort of formal uniform, dressed in worn denim and a checked shirt with the sleeves rolled up, teamed with an auburn mane and red beard—he definitely had that lumberjack vibe going on. Still, he wasn't the reason she was here. The only man she was interested in was the one who was giving her a job and a home.

'Yes. I'm taking over the café. Turning it into a chocolate shop. Now, if you don't mind, could you tell your boss I'm here, please?' She had hoped to have a shower and change before meeting her new employer, but, since no one seemed to know she was coming, Bonnie doubted her room was even ready.

'My boss?' He was openly laughing at her

now, only furthering the rise in her temper and need to get away from him.

'Yes, your boss. The duke. The owner of this castle, and the man I've been corresponding with.' Her sigh was full of frustration, exasperation, and all the stress she'd been going through for months. She didn't need any more hassle. Especially when this was supposed to be the new, shiny version of her life. Bonnie Abernathy 2.0.

The castle handyman-cum-butler-cum-pain-in-Bonnie's-backside carefully set the logs back down and stood up straight. 'That was probably my father. I'm sorry to say he passed away last month. I'm the new owner. The new Duke of Arbay.'

Although the smile had gone from his lips now, her tormentor continued to cause her anguish. A whole range of emotions and questions bombarded her at once as she processed this new information. She was sorry she'd never got to meet the man who'd given her so much confidence by believing in her and giving her a new start, and wondered what had happened to him. Most of all she was concerned about where the duke's death left her. Of course, it seemed selfish in the wake of this man losing his father to think about herself first, but without this position she had nothing. Her fate was in this man's hands. Definitely not a position she was relishing.

* * *

'I'm so sorry for your loss. He seemed like such a lovely man.'

Ewen had witnessed the shock, and the concern, cross the woman's face. These past weeks had been a whirlwind for him, so he knew how the news about his father's passing could disrupt a person's life. The least he could do was offer her a cup of tea to get over the shock.

'I'm Ewen. Ewen Harris.' He held out his hand, ignoring the comment about his father, and the fact he'd slammed the door in her face only moments earlier.

'Bonnie Abernathy,' she said, shaking his hand limply, her earlier fire seemingly having dissipated.

'Why don't you come in and I'll make us both a cuppa?' He opened the door, led her into the kitchen, and pulled out a chair for her before putting the kettle on.

Bonnie settled herself at the kitchen table whilst he tasked himself with finding some clean cups.

'I'm still trying to find my way around. It's a long time since I lived here.' Ewen opened and shut the cupboards looking for the good china, but making do with the chipped mugs he'd been using since moving back. He'd had more to sort out lately than appropriate dishware for unexpected visitors.

'Were you here when he died? Sorry. That's too personal a question. Forget I asked. I'm still trying to process the news.' She wrapped her hands around the mug of tea he poured for her, staring at it, apparently lost in her thoughts.

'It's okay. No, I wasn't here when it happened. I don't think anyone was. Heart attack in his sleep apparently.' Naturally he felt guilty about not being there, but Ewen's issues with his family went back further and deeper than just his father's passing.

'At least it was quick, and peaceful.'

'Yes. I'm thankful for that.'

Her analysis, whilst true, brought back thoughts of his brother Ruari's death, which might have been quick, but hadn't been peaceful. For any of them.

'So you're the new Duke of Arbay?'

'Yes. By default. My older brother, Ruari, died in a car accident twelve years ago.' Something he'd never forget, and something his parents had never forgiven him for. Because he'd been driving. It didn't matter that the road had been icy, that he'd only just passed his test—important points he'd reconciled with over the years and learned to forgive himself for. As far as they'd been concerned, he was responsible for the death of their firstborn.

It was that guilt, that blame, that had spurred him to leave for university in England, unable to live with his parents' blatant hatred, and why he'd never come home. Until now. Until forced by his father to live in this castle for a year before he could sell it and rid himself of the reminder of that terrible time for ever.

'I'm so sorry.'

'It was a long time ago.' He shrugged, not wishing to get into the sordid details with someone he'd just met.

'And you're here on your own? No other family? I thought you would at least have staff.'

Her forthright questions made him smile. It was refreshing to have someone be so upfront with him. Especially after Victoria, his partner of two years who'd apparently been pretending to love him to enjoy the benefits of his wealth. He'd become a success in his own right, creating an app that he'd sold later for millions. A one-stop shop for businesses that synced with their needs. Taking care of everything from contacting suppliers when the office copier ran out of ink, to linking directly to recruitment agencies when they needed staff. Basically, a digital office assistant.

Selling it, making his own fortune, had meant

he'd had no reason to come back home. It had suited everyone. He hadn't had to face the empty place where Ruari should've been, and his parents hadn't needed the reminder that Ewen existed. He got the impression they'd been happier believing they'd lost both sons in the crash than admitting they blamed Ewen and couldn't bear to look at him.

'My mother died ten years ago. I've been estranged from my parents for some time.' He hadn't come home for the funeral. Too busy in negotiations over the sale of his app. And, if he was honest, hadn't wanted to face his father. It would have felt hypocritical to turn up and mourn for his mother when they hadn't had any contact for years at that point. He'd only found out about his father because his solicitor had tracked him down. Only came back to tie up loose ends, then hopefully he'd be done with this place, and the memories for good.

He wasn't comfortable being here. In a way he was thankful for all the things keeping him too busy to dwell on the past, despite the inconvenience of it all. Dealing with his father's legal and financial affairs were practical things he could manage, but it was the emotional fallout from being back here that he feared.

He'd worked hard to be a success, to put the pain of his parents' rejection and the loss of his brother behind him. The death of his father, and his subsequent demands, had forced Ewen to live within these walls again, reliving those dark times, reminding him of the loneliness he'd felt at a time when he'd needed his family more than ever. Now he had no one.

'I'm sorry for your loss. I know something about being separated from parents. I haven't spoken to mine in quite some time.'

When he looked at her, expecting the reason, she simply shrugged. 'They didn't like my boyfriend. I left home to be with him, it didn't work out, but I don't want them to know they were right about him.'

He was about to offer his commiserations on the matter when she carried on, denying him the opportunity to butt in.

'Anyway, that's why I came here. For a new start.'

'I'm sorry things haven't worked out the way you expected. Do you have anything else in the pipeline?' He knew what it was like to have your life disrupted so suddenly and unexpectedly. A few weeks ago he'd been living in London with Victoria, not knowing he'd end up back in Scotland, single, and taking up residence on the family estate. The last surviving member of the Harris line. Although it was bad luck for Bonnie too that his father's death had clearly impacted on her plans, he was sure she'd find another job soon.

She didn't have the same conviction, sitting blinking at him, apparently stunned. 'No, I don't have a backup plan. This is it. My new start. Everything I own is in this case. I'm homeless, penniless, and apparently now jobless.'

Ewen frowned. He hadn't really paid much attention to the small trolley case until now, figuring it might have contained some small personal items she wanted for the café. It hadn't crossed his mind that she was carrying all her worldly possessions in it. To have so little told a story in itself, but she'd mentioned problems with a boyfriend and her parents, so it was obvious she'd gone through a rough time. Unfortunately, he was going through one of his own and didn't have room in his life to deal with someone else's troubles. Especially when she would have to move on.

'I don't understand…surely you had accommodation lined up to come here?' It didn't make any sense to him as to why it was his problem she had nowhere to go and no money to her name. He felt sorry for her, of course, but it wasn't any of his business, and he wanted it to remain that way. Victoria had made him wary of any beautiful woman now wishing to get close to him, in case they were only using him for his money and status. And here was a complete stranger turning up on his doorstep with a sob story, just as he'd become a duke and inherited the estate… He'd be a fool to be taken in a second time by a damsel in distress.

'You really know nothing about this?' She sighed, setting her cup down as though she were preparing to go into battle and needed her hands free.

'No. I've been busy with my father's funeral and sorting out his affairs. The staff are off until I'm ready to reopen to the public. There has been no mention of a new café manager, and quite frankly I don't see why your struggles are suddenly my problem. My father hired you, not me.'

Yes, he was being abrupt, but he still had a lot to sort through, and, technically, he was still grieving. It didn't matter that he and his father hadn't spoken in years, his death was still having a huge impact on his life, and there were things he needed space and time to process. He wasn't in the right frame of mind to start bringing strangers into the family home, or take on new staff. It was going to be a challenge dealing with the ones that were already employed here.

'I have a contract, written and verbal, to say I would have a place to stay here. I wouldn't have come otherwise.' She bit her lip before she said anything else, but Ewen had heard the rising panic in her voice and realised there was more going on than her being inconvenienced.

He wondered if it was something to do with the ex she'd mentioned. A break-up perhaps? Whilst she had his sympathy, something she probably didn't want or need, she wasn't his problem. He had enough of those to deal with and he didn't need to take on another one. Especially one in the form of an attractive brunette spitfire.

'That contract was with my father. I'm sorry but I'm not under any obligation to honour that.' Ewen was being harsh, but there was no room in his life for more complications, and that was exactly what this pretty stranger represented.

He didn't know why his father had decided to open the family home up to the public, or if he was even prepared to carry on with the tours. It didn't feel right taking on another member of staff when he wasn't sure what the future held for him or the castle. What Bonnie was asking for went beyond an extra pay cheque. After looking into the castle finances, he could tell they were sufficient to cover staff wages. His predicament had been whether or not to continue in that vein. And now Ms Abernathy had presented him with the added pressure of a possible resident.

It was difficult enough for him to be here after all this time, dealing not only with his past, but also his father's business affairs. On top of that, he was just getting over a break-up himself. He wasn't good company, not in the mood to have to pretend otherwise to a complete stranger who thought she had the right to live in the castle. The upheaval of his move here and his new, unwanted position was already stressful, and he didn't need the role of landlord/housemate added to his current workload. She should not be his responsibility.

Her full lips thinned into a determined line. 'I came here in good faith, hired by the Duke of Arbay to work in BenCrag Castle—'

'The previous Duke of Arbay...' he clarified.

'Nevertheless, the castle is still standing, as is the shop, and I'm here now. It would seem a little churlish on your part to send me away just because you're on a power trip.' She tilted her nose into the air, and, though she was fast becoming a pain in the proverbial, he kind of admired that fighting spirit in her.

Another red flag should he need it. The only positive thing to come out of this mess was that it was a distraction from his disastrous love life. He did not want a reason to like this pretty brunette, especially when she was trying to establish herself in this strange new life he'd been thrown into. When he inevitably sold up and moved on, he didn't want any ties or recriminations. The whole idea was to be finally done with this place and all the bad memories it represented. Not add more.

'Look, I don't even know if I'm going to open the café again. There's more going on in my life right now.'

'I appreciate that, but I'm sure your father wouldn't want to see me out on the street.' The sickly sweet smile as she batted her eyelashes was just as disarming as her warrior pose.

'That may be so, but he's not here, and he's left me to make the decisions regarding the castle's future.' Goodness knew why. Mrs McKenzie the housekeeper, Richard, the estate manager, or even the local students who volunteered in the gardens probably had more interest in that than he did. They would certainly have appreciated it more. Though he wasn't sure if even they would've agreed to letting an outsider live in the place rent-free.

Bonnie leaned forward. 'I don't want to make this a legal thing. I mean, we wouldn't want the press to get a hold of the story. It wouldn't look good for the new Duke of Arbay.'

Legally, he was sure she wouldn't have a leg to stand on if he decided to dispute the contract. After all, it was his father who had employed her. A legal battle would be lengthy and of no benefit to either of them in the end. However, he couldn't afford any bad publicity if he was going to open the castle again. Not when he already had a task ahead trying to win over local opinion of him. All anyone knew about him was that he was the driver of the car in the crash that killed his brother, and that he hadn't come home when either of his parents had died. It wasn't going to help his reputation if Bonnie went around telling people that he'd thrown her out on the street after his father had promised her a life here. She'd backed him into a corner, leaving only one option open to him.

'I'll give you a trial. If it doesn't work out, you'll move on.' He'd make sure it didn't work out, that she would hate being around him so much she'd move on of her own accord.

'Deal.' She was so quick to hold her hand out and shake on it, Ewen was beginning to have second thoughts about the whole idea. It felt as though he was losing control all over again.

'There aren't any rooms ready for you...' He was grasping for reasons to delay sharing his living space now, regardless that he'd agreed to it in the end.

Even though it was true. He was sleeping in his childhood bedroom and had yet to venture into any of the other rooms, including the one his father had passed away in.

'That's fine. Just point me in the right direction and I can sort one out for myself. I have a lot of work to do anyway if I'm going to open my chocolate shop. Do you have a date for the castle reopening?' Bonnie appeared brighter, sitting up taller in her chair, now that she had secured her job and accommodation again. Ewen, however, was becoming more unsettled by the second.

'No, I've just been taking one day at a time.' He'd been a little overwhelmed by the situation and his answer had been to dismiss the staff so he could be alone to deal with things. His go-to defence, harking back to Ruari's death when he'd had to work through the guilt and trauma of the accident by himself because his parents had been too wrapped up in their own grief to help.

'Well, I think it's about time we made some plans. Or else it's just going to be the two of us rattling around this big house for the rest of our days, and you don't want that, do you?'

No. No, he didn't. This fiery yet vulnerable stranger with big brown eyes who'd turned up on his doorstep had just upended his world all over again. Far from coming here to brood alone about the turn his life had taken, he had now found himself a housemate and a business to run.

Ewen didn't know what had prompted his father to make the decisions he'd made, agreeing to let a complete stranger move into the castle, and forcing his estranged son to stay in residence for a year. It felt as though he were still trying to punish him from beyond the grave. Testing him, pushing him to the limits of his patience, and waiting for him to break.

Only time would tell if he could rise to the occasion, or prove that the wrong son had died all those years ago.

CHAPTER TWO

'Morning,' Bonnie said brightly as she helped herself to the cereal in the cupboard and added a generous pouring of milk.

'Morning,' Ewen replied, barely looking up from his phone.

Regardless of his less than enthusiastic welcome, she joined him at the kitchen table. The one in the staff quarters, not the huge one upstairs she'd spotted in the dining hall on her quick tour of the castle that the duke was probably supposed to use. She felt more at home down in the modest farmhouse-style kitchen and she supposed he did too.

It had been an odd few days. Although they were living together, there was plenty of room to actively avoid each other, save for this room when they drifted together at mealtimes like this. She'd used the time to make her bedroom feel more like home, unpacking her few possessions and making the bed with the linen she'd found in the cupboard. Although she was aware she could be out on the street at any given moment.

She knew she didn't have a binding contract with Ewen, and it was clear he didn't want her here. In other circumstances she might not have pushed so hard, but without the job and the room here she had nothing. There was no way she was going back to the refuge when she'd so been looking forward to having a life of her own again. The centre had been her sanctuary, her escape from her ex, but it wasn't a home, living with a group of women all left traumatised and frightened by abusive partners.

At least here she could start over and not be reminded of the situation she'd been in for too long. Once she was earning enough money, able to put something by every month, she hoped she'd have enough for a deposit on her own place. All she had to do was not annoy Ewen too much so he'd let her stay until then. Not that he was making it easy. Every time he made it obvious that he didn't want her here, when it looked as though her new life was in jeopardy, she came out fighting.

They'd definitely got off on the wrong foot when she'd threatened legal action and bad press to force his hand, but she hadn't seen any other choice in that moment. His father had offered her a lifeline at a time when she was desperate for a new start, and she wasn't prepared to give it up without a fight. She'd had her fill of domineering men dictating what happened to her, and her time away from that oppressive situation with Ed had taught her she didn't have to put up with it.

'I'll replace the cereal and milk later when I do a shop. I just haven't had a chance to get any groceries yet. I don't want you to think I'm a bad housemate.' She was rabbiting to fill the silence between them that was only punctuated when she took a mouthful of bran flakes.

'Make sure you do. We're not housemates. You're more like a squatter I'm powerless to get rid of.' Ewen didn't look up, wearing that scowl that seemed to be omnipresent in her company.

She knew he'd just lost his father and had a lot to deal with here at the castle, but it was difficult not to be affected by his bad mood and clear dislike of her. Given her circumstances, she had to put up with it, but the tense atmosphere was something she'd hoped she'd never be forced to endure again. Just like living with Ed, one wrong move and she'd face the consequences. Except this time it was less about verbal and physical abuse, and more to do with losing her job and accommodation. Ewen held all the cards and she was powerless, save for her strong will, which had got her in the castle door at least. Hopefully once the other staff and visitors were trooping through his home, her presence would be a minor irritation he would eventually forget about altogether.

'Harsh, but perhaps I'll be able to win you over with my chocolate skills. There will never be a shortage of chocolate around here now. Speaking of which, I want to talk to you about plans for the shop. I wondered if there was a budget for the refurb? Although it's going to be a chocolate shop, I wondered if we should get one of those fancy coffee machines installed and encourage people to stay. Perhaps I could even branch out to making chocolate-based desserts.'

Ever since she'd agreed to take over the café her mind had been working overtime on what she could do. With this new independence she felt as though the world were her oyster, if only she had the money to achieve everything she wanted. Bonnie knew she was on thin ice with Ewen, but she was counting on him wanting the business to be a success too.

He glanced up at her this time, the scowl so deep she was sure it would leave a permanent indent. 'Let's not get carried away. We don't know how the chocolate shop is even going to go. I don't want to pour money into something that mightn't even be around in another year. Concentrate on what you're here for. Write a list for the basic equipment and ingredients you need, and we'll work from there.'

Finally putting his phone away, Ewen got up from the table and placed his dirty coffee cup in the sink.

Bonnie took a deep breath and counted to ten. 'Whatever you say, boss.'

She wasn't going to let his pessimism dampen her enthusiasm, or stop her from dreaming. For now, she'd bite her tongue and be grateful he'd conceded this far. Even if it had been under duress. It wouldn't do her any favours to butt heads with him again so soon. Besides, once he saw how good she was, Bonnie knew it would be easier to persuade him to invest more into the enterprise. In fact, once Ewen tasted her chocolates, he'd never want her to leave.

'I think the counter top and cash register we already have will do just fine for now,' Ewen insisted as he and Bonnie stood surveying the interior of the castle café a week later.

He could've done without the distraction and complication of having her living in the house with him. Not only was he tortured with the sight of her in the mornings wearing little more than a dressing gown that barely covered her round backside, there was no escape from her constant pushing for big changes in the castle.

It was understandable that she would be ambitious, wanting to make the most of this opportunity, but he needed to be cautious. In both his personal and professional life.

He didn't want to be attracted to any woman at present, and certainly not a stranger wanting him to invest his money in her dream. Victoria had taught him a hard-learned lesson to be cautious when it came to his money and relationships. For all he knew, Bonnie was just another gold-digger deploying her feminine wiles to make him lose all common sense and think with other parts of his anatomy rather than his head. She'd made it clear she had no money, and from the outside he must have seemed like a stable financial prospect. Victoria had obviously thought so when they'd got together. It was all very well appreciating a woman's beauty and spirit, but he needed to be cautious about even entertaining the idea of getting close to someone again, to protect his heart, and his assets.

On a practical, business level, if things went to plan he was going to be selling the castle as soon as the conditions of his father's will had been met. He'd already made enquiries with an estate agent about putting the place on the market. So it would be pointless investing more money into the business now, and he definitely didn't need to do it to impress Bonnie when he needed to give her reason to leave. And soon.

'Can I at least redecorate?' she huffed, arms folded, clearly not impressed by his answer.

'Sure. Why do you think I'm here?' He hoisted the tin of paint he'd stashed there earlier onto the table.

Bonnie peered at it, wrinkling her nose in disgust. 'Beige?'

'Yes, beige.'

'I don't get a say?'

'You're the manager, not the owner. The place still needs to be in keeping with the rest of the castle. Nothing ostentatious, but subtle. We don't know how business is going to go, so I don't want to be left with sparkly pink walls and rainbow-coloured carpet if this doesn't work out.' It would make it difficult to sell on to any potential buyers.

'What makes you think I would be so OTT?'

Ewen looked her up and down, taking in the azure-blue dress she was wearing, emblazoned with bright yellow sunflowers, and the matching yellow wedges on her feet. He loved that she was expressing herself, her vivid wardrobe livening up the interior of the otherwise drab building. However, he had to draw the line when it came to the castle aesthetics.

'Okay, point taken, as long as you don't expect

me to start wearing some generic dull uniform. I've had my fill of being told what to wear and how to behave.'

The comment grabbed a hold of Ewen and wouldn't let go. He wasn't going to pry, but Bonnie's past had clearly left its mark on her. He couldn't imagine anyone trying to tame her, or wanting to. Perhaps whatever had happened to her was partly to blame for them butting heads, along with his frustration at being forced to live with her in a place he couldn't wait to escape from.

If she'd been with someone who'd dominated her, it was no wonder she was rebelling against Ewen putting his foot down and asking her to fall into line with his wishes. He understood her blatant need to assert her independence, he'd done the same when he'd moved away from home. Keen to escape the burden of guilt his parents had tried to heap upon him, he'd moved quickly to start a new life for himself at university, almost becoming a completely different person in the process. He was no longer a naïve, privileged rich kid, but a jaded, older-than-his-years man who'd had to be proactive about securing a financial future away from his family.

However, it was also important for him now to remind Bonnie he was her boss, or he'd make a rod for his own back in the future. Victoria had spent most of their time together splurging his cash for her own benefit, leaving him with the bills when she moved on elsewhere. He wasn't prepared to let that happen a second time.

'You can wear what you like. If it makes you happy you can put whatever paintings you want on the walls.' A few pictures could always be taken down and wouldn't cost the earth. He hoped the compromise would keep her happy and give her some sense of control over her work environment.

For a split second her eyes lit up and he thought he'd won her over. Then she pulled a face, clearly not wanting to seem as though she was caving too easily.

'You're *too* generous.'

'I know,' he said, ignoring the blatant sarcasm. 'That's why I'm devoting my spare time to painting the place myself.'

She rolled her eyes. 'Because you're *so* generous and not at all a tight-ass.'

That made him laugh. He didn't know how, or why, anyone would want to dampen Bonnie's spirit, but he was glad she'd broken free from whoever had tried to control her. She was certainly going to keep him on his toes around here. Since the split from Victoria he'd felt as though he was alone in the world, his entire family now dead save for him. But he wasn't sure if it was any easier for him having Bonnie in situ. He'd become accustomed to being on his own, only making decisions concerning himself. Now he was beginning to feel responsible for her too. More than that, he was beginning to like her, and he couldn't afford to let either get in the way of his plans.

The staff had begun to filter back to the castle to get ready for the reopening—the grounds-keeper, and the estate manager, as well as maintenance—but they went home at the end of the day. Though he didn't actively seek Bonnie out at night, her room was only a few doors down from his in the part of the castle that was closed off to visitors, so he often heard her walking in the hallway, or singing to herself. Enough for him to remember he wasn't alone with his ghosts. Not that he wanted to get too used to having her around when he intended to sell the place and move on when he could. Something that would certainly not endear him to Bonnie, but he hoped by that time she would be ready to move on to bigger and better things too. This was merely a stopgap for both of them.

'Feel free to help. It will get done quicker with two of us.' He opened the lid on the paint and offered her a paint roller.

'No, thanks. I've plenty to do in the kitchen. Recipes to finesse, chocolate to temper and sample. You know, all the real hard work.' She grinned before turning on her sunshine-yellow wedges and sashaying towards the kitchen at the back of the small room.

Ewen couldn't help but admire the sway of her hips in the figure-skimming jersey dress and the proud way she carried herself. This was a woman reclaiming her confidence and the person she was. Someone he was beginning to admire more with every interaction, regardless of the inconvenience. When he let his eyes dip to the fullness of her backside he knew it was time to occupy his thoughts elsewhere.

He covered the floor with the dustsheet he'd brought, picked up the paint roller, and did his best to block out the sound of her happy singing in the kitchen.

Bonnie had arranged the kitchen the way she wanted it, made some of her staple chocolate truffles and started to build her basic stock for opening day. She could give out a variety of milk, dark and white chocolates as samples to any potential customers, though she wanted to work on something special. A signature creation specially for the castle. Something with whisky perhaps, linking to the Scottish heritage, or a lavender base as a nod to the purple beauty in abundance by the castle walls. She wanted to put her little chocolate shop on the map. With visitors paying an entrance fee to get into the castle, she wasn't likely to get repeat custom yet, relying on rich tourists flocking in en masse. So she needed something eye-catching and palate-pleasing to get them to spend their money.

Her plan was to eventually have a website selling online, maybe even doing personalised corporate orders. Whatever it took to make the business a success and make a name for herself in the chocolate world. Then all of those weekends and holidays she'd spent working in her father's business wouldn't have been wasted after all. And it would certainly boost her self-confidence to have a purpose again.

Of course, she'd have to get it past Ewen first. A minor hiccup. Despite his gruff exterior Ewen would do what was best for the shop, and the castle. After all, she'd managed to persuade him to let her stay and work here. He'd even spent the day painting the shop walls that unattractive beige colour, which she was going to be sure to cover up as best she could with the permitted artwork she would now be on the hunt for.

Her stomach grumbled. They'd worked through lunch, but since she'd spent all day in the kitchen she didn't fancy standing making dinner down in the depths of the castle staff quarters.

'Do you fancy a takeaway?' she shouted across the short distance between them, leaving her spotless kitchen to seek out her boss. 'Although, we should probably eat it somewhere else. The smell of paint fumes is making my eyes water.'

Although they weren't the closest of housemates, primarily because he made it obvious he didn't want her there, it made sense to share the meal. Not only could they split the cost, at a time when she was counting every penny, but it saved on waste. She wasn't the sort of person who liked to microwave takeaway leftovers the next day. Also, despite their clash of personalities at times, they'd got along fine today.

If she was honest, the company would be nice for a change too. It had been a while since she'd shared a meal with anyone, and even longer since she'd enjoyed one without the threat of her companion's temper spoiling it. She could handle Ewen's tendency towards grumpiness if it meant she had someone to talk to other than the walls for one evening. He'd almost been congenial today, even if he was only painting the shop to save money.

Bonnie was wondering how he'd managed to work all day without getting high or passing out, when she saw him sitting slumped over one of the tables, his head in his hands.

'Ewen? Are you okay?' Her heart sank at the thought that something had happened to him and she'd been completely oblivious.

Yes, she'd battled against him on nearly every decision since her arrival, but that was only to be expected given her limited history with men. To have another male telling her what she could and couldn't do had been a trigger, inciting that need for her to fight for her independence. Okay, he was her boss, and, as such, she had to make compromises, but she was damned if she'd go back to being that submissive woman who'd simply fall into line or face the consequences. She hadn't realised she'd become so feisty in the short space of time since she'd left her ex until meeting Ewen. There was a lot to begrudgingly thank him for, even if she had backed him into a corner, and she certainly didn't want him to come to any harm.

It was only when she came to touch him on the arm she realised he was sitting in front of his laptop, his earbuds in, oblivious to the outside world.

He jumped when she made contact with him and pulled out his earbuds. 'Sorry. I didn't hear you.'

'I didn't mean to scare you. I thought you'd passed out from the paint fumes. I didn't spot the laptop, or the earbuds.'

'I was just going through the calendar for the year trying to figure out how I'm going to honour all of the bookings my father apparently took. Is there something I can do for you?' He closed the laptop as though there was something he didn't want her to see, or no longer wanted to deal with.

'I thought you might like to get some takeaway rather than cooking tonight. It's been a long, hard day for us both and we could do with putting our feet up.' There hadn't been much interaction between them outside castle and shop business, but ordering food for one seemed a step too far. They weren't in high school, they weren't going to catch anything by being in the same room, and she was sure they could manage a civil conversation over some fast food. It might even begin to feel as if she was back in the real world.

Although she'd left Ed, moved on from the refuge, and found a place of her own—albeit part of a castle—she had yet to fully immerse herself in her new reality. She didn't know if she could still function as a human being. If she'd ever feel comfortable around people again, or if she was always going to feel on edge. Waiting for something bad to happen.

Making small talk with Ewen would be a start. A gentle lead in to dealing with members of the public. Having worked in retail at her parents' place when she was a teenager, she was aware it required her to be amiable and approachable. As the face of the chocolate shop at the castle, she had nowhere to hide. After years of her being in the background, cowed by her partner, running a shop was like being thrown into the deep end in terms of socialising again. A challenge she was more than willing to take on when it meant finally getting her life back under her control.

'Sure. I've got some menus downstairs if you want to have a look and decide what you want? I can make the call and we can eat it in the lounge. It'll be much more comfortable, and warmer, than the kitchen.'

It also meant crossing over into Ewen's private quarters. So far their interactions had been confined to the communal kitchen and the parts of the castle open to visitors. She had her own room and en suite bathroom but, most likely, he had a few rooms to call his own that were closed to the public.

Her hesitation was based purely on the idea of breaching that invisible line between work and their personal lives. They'd had their differences of opinion, but he'd never forced her to submit to his will. She liked that they were able to compromise, that, despite initial appearances, he was a reasonable man. He was also going through a difficult time and she was sure that had a lot to do with his mood. Something she could easily relate to—she was more defensive than usual too.

Even though she knew she was safe around Ewen, that he was no threat to her, it was still a big step to socialise with a man alone. It had crossed her mind when coming to live here that she'd find it difficult to live with another man in any circumstances. That she'd never be able to let her guard down in case someone else tried to take advantage of her. Or hurt her. But he'd given her a job and somewhere to live when he really didn't have to, and she got the impression he was every bit as alone as she was.

'Okay. Let me get changed first. I'm covered in chocolate. I'll see you down there in fifteen minutes.' It gave her a little breathing space, time to regroup, before venturing into unknown territory.

Although she knew sharing some food with her boss was nothing to fear, or be anxious about, it was another big step out of her comfort zone. One she knew she needed to take in order to move on.

CHAPTER THREE

EWEN JUMPED IN the shower and scrubbed off as much of the paint as he could see, then donned a pair of jeans and a clean tee shirt. Victoria would be mortified by his wardrobe these days, though he'd found it quite liberating to swap city suits for comfy casuals. He supposed once the castle was reopened he'd have to dress the part, but he drew the line at wearing a kilt to keep the tourists happy. A shirt and tie would have to suffice. He wanted to look smart for his new role as the duke, and in control of what was happening on the estate. Even if that seemed out of reach at present.

The sound of Bonnie rapping on the door forced him out of his reverie. Despite being in the same space, they'd managed to avoid each other for most of the day. That was what had made her suggestion seem so out of left-field. Yet, he'd agreed before he'd had time to think it through properly, desperate for some company.

He'd known moving to the castle was going to

be an upheaval, but he hadn't realised he'd end up here alone, with nothing, or no one to go back to. Once Victoria had gone he'd sold up, hadn't seen the point of keeping an expensive, empty apartment in London for a year. It meant whenever he was finally able to get rid of the castle and the other problems his father had left, he had nowhere else to go. In that sense, he understood where Bonnie was coming from. He knew, unlike her, he had options, money to go anywhere, but he had no friends or family around him. Another thing they seemed to have in common. He supposed it wouldn't hurt either of them to have some company once in a while.

The sight of her when he opened the door made him smile. Her hair was still damp from her shower, the curly ends wetting the shoulders of her slouchy grey sweatshirt, and she'd swapped her dress for a pair of comfy jogging bottoms. Clearly marking the distinction between work and play. Victoria had always dressed to the nines, with full make-up and coiffed hairdo, which was her prerogative, but had made him feel slightly on edge. As though he always had to be on display too, in case he let her down by appearing in an outfit she didn't deem acceptable. At least he could relax tonight.

'Hey. Come on in.' He opened the door to let Bonnie in. It seemed a bit strange when they were ostensibly living in the same house, if in separate areas. Housemates who rarely interacted.

'Sorry I don't have a bottle of wine or a bunch of flowers to offer for your hospitality,' she said, ducking inside. It was then he noticed her pink fluffy slipper boots. She really was going for comfort tonight. At least it showed she felt she could be herself around him, and it made it easier for Ewen to relax, knowing she wasn't likely to mistake this evening for anything other than a meal together. Getting the sense that she'd recently gone through a break-up too, he didn't imagine either of them were interested in a relationship of any kind. Not that having dinner with one another constituted a commitment beyond cultivating a more harmonious working environment.

He supposed he should be happy that he seemed to raise her hackles every time they spoke. It would make it easier in terms of scaring her off, and relieving him of any responsibility towards her. But he was emotionally drained by recent events and simply wanted a quiet dinner in some company for a change. At least if they were eating, they wouldn't get caught in another verbal battle of wills.

'No need. I have some wine here and I've had so many sympathy flowers delivered recently I could open my own florist shop. Besides, technically we live together, so dinner isn't that big a deal.'

'You're right. Now, where are those menus? Because I need to eat.' With that, she walked on into the lounge and threw herself down onto the settee, making herself at home.

Ewen did the same, pulling out his phone and the stack of menus he'd found earlier. It was the most normal he'd felt in weeks.

They'd opted for Italian in the end. Bonnie figured the carb overload of pasta and creamy sauces was the ultimate comfort food they both needed. Though she might not need to eat again for another week.

'Would you like some more wine?' Ewen held up the rest of the bottle of white they'd already enjoyed with their dinner, and she nodded as he topped up their glasses.

Regardless of being in a castle, surrounded by antique furniture and valuable paintings, it felt like a cosy night in. Normal. Not a night in a room no bigger than a cell, sharing a building with other women afraid of their own shadows, too traumatised to socialise. Nor another evening trying to be as invisible as possible so as not to antagonise her other half by simply breathing. Neither scenario had been any sort of life, and though no one could call this exciting, it was exactly what she needed right now. Simply chilling out with good food, good wine and good company. Bonnie couldn't remember the last time she'd felt so contented, and relaxed.

That was when the doubt crows began to circle, pecking her head with their sharp beaks to remind her that it couldn't last. Her whole life had been dictated by men telling her what to do. Ewen was her boss. Tonight was nice, but, by the very nature of their relationship, he had the power. Something he'd demonstrated already, and once the castle was back up and running as a business it was going to be tough for her to fall into line again. Who knew how long this new way of life was going to last? Ultimately, her fate was still at the mercy of another man, and, after everything she'd been through, that didn't sit well with her.

'Uh-oh,' Ewen said, leaning forward, his forehead wrinkled into a frown.

'What is it?' Her stomach knotted at the thought that she'd done something wrong. Something to upset him. A throwback to the life she'd lived with her ex, when she'd constantly been on eggshells, waiting to find out what she'd done to trigger his anger.

'I can see you're lost in your thoughts, and

they don't look to me as though they're very happy ones.'

She offered him a reassuring smile. Something else she was used to doing to make the peace. However, on this occasion, Ewen's observation, combined with his concern for her, made it a genuine reaction for once.

'Just thinking about things, and people, I left in the past.'

'And that's where they should stay. Although, it's not that easy when they're still dictating your everyday behaviour, is it?' Ewen knocked back the rest of his wine, almost as though he was trying to blot something out too.

'What makes you say that?' Bonnie took a sip from her glass, her hand shaking, jolted by his apparent insight into her innermost thoughts. She wanted to know if she'd done anything to give him the impression she'd been left dealing with a deep-seated trauma by her ex, or if he'd had his own experiences.

He set his glass on the coffee table, creating a barrier between them, and leaned forward, his forearms resting on his lap. 'When you arrived, you were homeless, penniless, and defensive. I know it's none of my business, but I get the impression you went through more than a break-up. Whatever happened, I do know how incredibly brave it was to come here and start over.'

'Thank you, but I'm fine,' she whispered, trying to hold it together. The reminder of how much it had taken for her to walk away in the end, and the fact he was acknowledging that, were bringing up all sorts of emotions.

She hadn't intended to share anything about that with anyone, never mind her new boss. As well as being painful to recall those memories, it was humiliating to share the details of that relationship. Ewen had seen her only at her fighting best after counselling had bolstered her confidence. She didn't want him to see her any differently. Certainly not as the weak woman who'd let herself be used and abused for way too long. Yes, she knew now that she wasn't responsible for Ed's behaviour, but even she didn't recognise the young woman who'd been taken in by a pretty face and some attention. These days she was more worldly-wise, not to mention cynical.

Only the women at the refuge had known what she'd been through. By that stage she wasn't in contact with any of her old friends, or her parents. She'd had no one to turn to, and no one to tell her she'd done the right thing, the brave thing, at the loneliest, most frightening time of her life. The help she'd received from the charity had saved her. But she was trying to move on and didn't want to keep looking back. From now on she had to be more careful about her choice of words around Ewen.

Ewen sat back in his seat again, giving her back the personal space she needed in that moment. 'I didn't think I'd ever come back here myself.'

'Oh?' It was the first time Ewen had opened up to her about his personal life. Whether it was the effect of the alcohol, the cosy atmosphere that had developed between them tonight, or that he felt he needed to share something of himself to even the score, Bonnie didn't know. But she was ready to listen. It was clear he wasn't happy about being here. For someone who'd just inherited land, a title, and his father's fortune, he seemed as though he had the weight of the world on his shoulders.

'I've been estranged from my family since I was eighteen. I went to university and very rarely came back. I made a life of my own. My father's death forced me to return, to take up the role I never wanted.' The pressure he was feeling was there to see in his slumped shoulders, and, now she was looking closely, there was a smudge under his blue eyes that told of his sleepless nights.

'Perhaps this was your father's way of making amends?' Of course, she didn't know the circumstances, nor was she privy to anyone else's thoughts or motivations, but it was a possibility. Whatever had happened between them had been serious enough for Ewen to stay away all these years, but his father leaving everything to him in his will seemed to her to be an act of contrition.

Ewen shrugged. 'Then why not come to me before he died? Why lumber me with all of these bookings to honour? I've got a wedding, craft fairs, and then there's the matter of the annual ball...what would make him take on these commitments? He didn't need the money, so I don't understand why he'd want so many strangers traipsing through the house.'

'From the couple of times I spoke to him, he seemed lonely. When I enquired about accommodation he jumped at the chance to have me here. I think he was looking forward to having someone else in residence. Unlike you.' She dared to tease him, watching for his reaction. Relieved when he didn't appear to take offence. It was refreshing, and novel, to be able to joke around without fearing any potential consequences.

'It's nothing personal. I'm not really the best person to be around right now. I broke up with my girlfriend before I came here. Then, of course, there's the knowledge that I will never see my father again, that we won't have a chance to reconcile. If this wasn't one last chance to dig the knife in deeper...'

Bonnie felt for him. She knew what it was like to have no one to turn to for support. To feel utterly alone and full of regret. She'd been so wrapped up in her own personal issues, she hadn't recognised Ewen might be struggling too. That he was hurting just as much as she was, and perhaps that was why they'd clashed so much at the beginning, only to spend the next few days in isolation licking their respective wounds. She hoped going forward they'd be able to give each other more consideration.

It made her think too about her own family circumstances. Of how she'd left things with her parents, and how she'd been too hurt, too embarrassed by what had happened with Ed to get back in touch. She didn't know what it would do to her if they died without ever having the chance to build some bridges. Perhaps when she was feeling stronger, was more settled in her job, she could offer an olive branch and see if there was a relationship worth salvaging. Unlike Ewen, she still had a chance to reconcile, or get some closure on that part of her life.

'I haven't spoken to my parents for eight years. They knew the man I was seeing was bad news, but I thought they just didn't want me to be happy. That they were trying to control me. Of course, now I know they were right, but I don't want them to know that. It sounds petty, but I'm not ready to face the "we told you so" conversations.'

A lot of hurtful things were said on both sides out of anger and pain. In hindsight, and with a more mature attitude to the situation, Bonnie knew they were only acting out of love. Perhaps all the control issues she'd had with them came down to that—they'd only wanted her to be safe, even if the way they'd gone about it had been difficult to take. She was worried that though she might be ready to forgive and regret, they might not be. They might decide life was better without her in it, and that rejection would be too much for someone still so vulnerable and fragile.

'Trust me, you don't want to be left with regrets. Those conversations you have in your head, of all the things you should've said, how they might have reacted, how different things could have been, will drive you mad. I'm sure they just want you to be safe. Maybe try reaching out with a text or a call first before confronting them face to face.'

What Ewen was saying wasn't unreasonable. A text message wouldn't be too painful. Just a hello to start with, to see if they responded, should suffice for now. As soon as she worked up the courage to send it. After all, she'd done the hard part by leaving the man who had physically and emotionally caused her harm. She should be ready to tackle anything.

'I might do that. Thanks.'

'No problem. At least it will make me feel as though I've achieved something here if I save you from making the same mistakes I did.'

'So what are you going to do about the bookings?' Although she was naturally curious about what had happened to cause such a split in the family, she wasn't ready to share details of her own personal life in return. It was better to focus on the future instead of looking back, especially when he was so concerned about what he was taking on at BenCrag. It was a huge responsibility to pick up where his father had left off, and he seemed convinced he was going to fail.

Even though Ewen had been estranged from his family, to her mind his father had passed on the reins to him because he'd believed he was capable. The best man for the job. All that was needed was for Ewen to have the same belief in himself. She would understand if he didn't honour the bookings, but she didn't see him as someone who gave up at the first sign of trouble. Hopefully he'd realise that continuing with his father's business plans was the right thing to do.

He stretched out his legs with a sigh, crossing his feet at the ankles, and folding his arms across his chest. A real mixed message about being open, and closed, at the same time. He was conflicted. It was only natural when making the big calls. She'd had her fair share of wobbles and worries until she'd eventually worked up the courage to pick up her ready-packed bag and leave her ex.

'That's the million-dollar question, isn't it? If I cancel, it'll ruin the castle's, and the family's, reputation. Not to mention letting down my father. If I honour these bookings, even though I'll have no clue what I'm doing, it's extremely likely I'll let a lot of people down anyway. It's a lose-lose situation for me.'

It might seem like an insurmountable mountain to climb, but if Bonnie had taken that attitude, she would never have made the break from her toxic relationship. Dealing with huge life-changing decisions wasn't easy, but she was willing to help. They needed visitors, and good word of mouth, for the sake of both their jobs. 'Let's start with the wedding…when is it?'

'Next Saturday,' he said with a grimace, which Bonnie matched.

'And you haven't been in contact with the bride and groom yet?' The way he'd been stressing over forthcoming events led her to believe he had yet to make contact with any of the parties involved.

'No. I know, I should've dealt with it, but I really don't know where to start.'

'Well, it's definitely too short notice to cancel a wedding party now. I'd suggest contacting them, telling them the castle is under new ownership and asking for all relevant details about the day. You know, timings, caterers, florists—find out what's already been arranged. Have a look and see if your father has any info too. He's bound to have a record of these things. The housekeeper and estate manager will have information too, I'm sure. Use them. They've probably dealt with this kind of thing before. You don't have to do this alone, Ewen.'

As they were preparing to reopen the castle, the staff had begun to filter back to make it presentable. Bonnie had met a few of the key staff, and they'd been helpful and welcoming. They also seemed to be aware of her appointment on staff too, which helped her feel less like an intruder. She was sure they'd all pull together to make a success of whatever was planned.

Ewen was nodding his head to everything she said. 'You're right. I didn't give anyone a chance to tell me what was in the castle diary, sending everyone away the moment I got here. Hopefully, they won't hold that against me.'

'I can only imagine, given how warmly you greeted me.' She raised an eyebrow, wondering how many other feathers he'd ruffled in the process of becoming the new duke. 'However, you're grieving. I'm sure people will make allowances for that. I did. Because at the end of the day, we're all making our livelihood from this place.'

Despite her honesty, she thought she saw a fleeting look of disappointment cross Ewen's features as she spoke. As much as she was sure everyone on staff loved the castle, they were still employees. They relied on it being a success to get their wages and pay their bills. Not everyone was lucky enough to come from a privileged, wealthy family.

'I deserve that rap over the knuckles.' He stretched out his arm, and Bonnie gave him a playful slap across the back of the hand.

'Yes, you do, but I wasn't on my best behaviour either, so let's leave it in the past.' She'd come out swinging the second he'd confronted her on his doorstep, lashing out like the injured animal she was. Although she still had a long way to go, her defences were gradually being lowered, the claws retracting. That was the only reason she would ever have agreed to be here in his apartment tonight.

With the new truce in place, Ewen clapped his hands together. 'So, any suggestions to make the day special and really put us on the map again?'

Bonnie blinked at him, wondering how she'd managed to get him to get on board so quickly, and get herself involved.

'Well, as long as there are no dietary requirements I need to know about, perhaps I could make some sort of chocolate centrepiece for the reception. It could add something special, and advertise the new shop.' It would also give her more than truffles to showcase her expertise with, if they ever did venture into online marketing with the chocolate shop.

'You could do that? It would give me something positive to lead with when I talk to the couple, in case they're worried about the changes going on.' Ewen was suddenly enthused, sitting up straighter in his chair, his blue eyes bright, and there was a new nervous energy about him. As though, instead of his dreading the forthcoming nuptials, she'd given him something to look forward to.

She didn't want to give him false hope that one chocolate sculpture was going to save the day, but she liked to see him looking more energised about business prospects at the castle. The last thing she needed was the new heir to decide it was more hassle than he wanted to deal with and sell the whole place on. Bonnie was prepared to put in whatever work it took to maintain her new independence. Even if that meant forging a new alliance with her boss. Now it seemed as though she was very much part of the upcoming wedding, and its success…

For the first time since he'd taken over at the castle, Ewen was feeling optimistic. Sitting down with Bonnie tonight had given him a new perspective on things, as well as a chance to get a few things off his chest. Although he hadn't gone into specific details about his break-up with Victoria, Bonnie was the first person he'd actually had a conversation with about it.

Bonnie had also helped to allay some of his fears over the wedding booked for next week, on a practical level. When he'd been confronted with those bookings he'd gone into something of a tailspin, wondering how he was going to pull it all off. Not realising he didn't have to do it all on his own. His father certainly hadn't. He had a team around him who, as Bonnie had pointed out, would have experience dealing with these things. Since leaving home he'd been so used to doing everything for himself, it hadn't occurred to him that there was help available. All he had to do was work with everyone, take their ideas and comments on board, as he had done with Bonnie tonight. It could make the world of difference.

She already had.

He might not have wanted her here, but she'd been a help to him tonight.

'I can't wait to see what you come up with for the centrepiece.' As an app designer, he had some level of creativity, but he was looking forward to seeing what Bonnie's imagination conjured up.

This was clearly important to her. She wanted to make the chocolate shop a success, as much as he did the castle reopening. Goodness knew he didn't want to be seen as a failure in the eyes of his father's friends and peers, when they'd probably heard all sorts about him over the years. None of it likely to be good, given the non-relationship he'd had with his parents. This could be his one and only chance to prove himself, to finally be an asset to his family.

'I'm a bit rusty. It's been a while since I tackled anything on this scale, and I was never allowed to freestyle in my father's shop. With that level of jeopardy, it should make things interesting to say the least.'

Ewen knew she was teasing, but he didn't mind. He could see her testing boundaries with him, pushing to see how he reacted, no doubt ready to fight back if necessary. She was being provocative, wary of the sort of person he might be, but he liked her honesty. Victoria's betrayal had made him cautious about trusting anyone again, but Bonnie was acting in her own best interests as well as his. This new life was all she had and she wanted to protect it. So he was trusting her not to mess things up, for both their sakes.

CHAPTER FOUR

'YES, I'LL LOOK for it later, Mrs McKenzie.' Ewen took a note of his housekeeper's request for his father's address book. It was bound to be in the study, but he had other matters to attend to.

'It's very important, Your Grace. That book contains all of your father's important contacts. We'll need that for the guest list. You know, for the ball.' Her not-so-subtle hint that he'd yet to make a decision on that particular bugbear stopped him mid tread on the staircase.

'Please, call me Ewen. I haven't agreed to that yet. One thing at a time.' He'd prefer to see how this wedding went before he committed to anything more. At least the happy couple had hired a wedding planner who had a very detailed schedule planned down to the last tea rose, so all he had to do was turn up and add an air of nobility to proceedings.

Of course, they needed to ensure the castle was looking its best, but Mrs McKenzie and the estate manager were employing all of their skills to make that happen. Everything seemed to be in hand. Except for the spectacular chocolate centrepiece he'd promised to deliver, which had yet to appear.

'But—but all the residents so look forward to coming here to celebrate every year. It's tradition.' The matronly figure who'd been here when he was a child looked distraught at the very notion celebrations would be postponed. He didn't want to upset her when she was helping him find his feet at the castle, but neither did he want to give her, or the rest of the village, false hope.

'Look, Mrs McKenzie, I appreciate everything you're doing for me. I really do. But hosting a ball is totally different from someone using the castle for a wedding venue. The wedding planner has organised everything for this, co-ordinated the deliveries and the caterers. I'm merely decoration for this.'

'I would help you, as I'm sure Ms Abernathy would. She seems very keen to be part of life here at the castle.' It appeared Bonnie already had a fan, though it came as no surprise when she'd really thrown herself into the castle re-opening.

As well as stocking the display cabinet with all sorts of tasty treats, she'd been greeting their visitors with some samples as they arrived for the castle tours. He had no doubt she would jump at the chance to help him host a ball here too, but Ewen wasn't sure if he wanted that. The ball was a gathering for all of the nearby residents, along with some of his father's high status friends. Ewen didn't want to be a hypocrite, throwing an elaborate party and befriending the locals when he planned on selling up at some point. Getting to know people and their circumstances would make it more than a simple business decision and he didn't want any more obstacles in his path. Once his year here was up he'd be moving on somewhere for a completely new start, with no obligations or ties. He certainly didn't need to carry any more guilt with him. It was better that the sale went ahead without any emotional attachments that could potentially throw a spanner in the works.

'Speaking of which… I need to go and make sure she's ready for the big reveal on Saturday. Once the wedding is over, we'll talk again about the ball. And yes, I'll look for the address book,' he called over his shoulder, already continuing his ascent towards the chocolate shop, leaving the sighing housekeeper far behind him.

Much like the rest of the castle now, the shop was empty when Ewen got there. It wasn't surprising, as they'd stopped admitting visitors an hour ago, but they'd been open for a few days and business hadn't exactly been brisk. Even though he wasn't intending to stay beyond the required amount of time stipulated in his father's will, he still needed it to be a viable business to make a profitable sale, and it was concerning. More so if Bonnie wasn't getting the sales she'd hoped for either.

He'd invested in the chocolate shop, buying whatever equipment and ingredients she needed. But it was more than a financial issue. He wanted the shop to be a success for Bonnie's sake. It went against the notion of chasing her away so he could have peace of mind, but he got the impression she needed that confidence boost. The more time they spent around one another, the more he was able to see past her defensive exterior and see that vulnerable centre. Like him, she'd clearly been wounded, and he reckoned they both needed a break.

With no sign of her out front, he walked towards the kitchen. Just in time to hear a clatter on the floor and a short burst of expletives. He gave a cursory knock on the door before he opened it and found Bonnie on her hands and knees on the floor picking up broken shards of chocolate.

'Is everything all right in here?' he asked, eyeing the counter tops littered with trays of chocolate and used equipment. It looked as though a bomb had literally gone off in a sweet shop.

Bonnie shoved her hair out of her eyes to look

up at him, smudging chocolate onto her fore-head in the process. 'Just dandy. I've lost the castle wall.'

She gathered up the two large flat, broken slabs of chocolate and deposited them into the waste bin with a heavy thud.

'Okay…dare I ask how it's going?' He needed to know, after making promises to the wedding party, that they'd produce something spectacular in chocolate. With a lack of any structure in sight, and the fact she had yet to even mention what she was working on, his anxiety levels were rising dramatically.

Bonnie glared at him, then held out her hands like a disgruntled magician's assistant pointing out the mess surrounding her. 'I need about six pairs of hands to get this done. Every time I try to stick the walls together, another one falls down. I need something to hold them in place whilst I work.'

'What is it you're making?' He wandered around the worktop to have a closer look, where he could see it wasn't simply a mess of broken chocolate and dreams, but very carefully crafted slabs and domes sitting waiting to be assembled.

'Can't you tell?' She grinned, so he didn't feel so bad that he'd failed to recognise whatever it was she'd been slogging over.

'I…er…'

'It's the castle.' She turned the two-dimensional shapes into 3D, lifting up some of the slabs to form walls, and give him a better idea of what she had planned.

It *was* the castle. He could see the turrets waiting to be added, and she'd even formed a tiny replica of the door knocker on the original oak front door.

'That's amazing.' Although there was a long way to go before completion, he could see the vision she'd had for the final piece. A complete scale model of the castle. All made out of chocolate.

'It might be, if I can get the walls to stick together,' she said, carefully laying down the slabs again.

'Can I do anything to help?'

'Are you serious?'

Ewen nodded. 'We're on the same team, remember? Just tell me where you want me.'

He took off his suit jacket, hung it on the back of a chair, and gave his hands a quick wash and dry at the sink.

'Great! If you could hold this, and this, it leaves me free to try and stick them together.' Bonnie guided his hands with hers to hold two of the larger slabs at an angle.

Her touch was soft, but firm, showing him where he needed to be. It was the closest they'd managed to stand to each other since she'd arrived. Her chestnut hair tickled his nose and he inhaled a deep breath, taking in her scent of vanilla and cocoa, and everything that reminded him of his happier childhood days. Back when his mother used to bake chocolate-chip cookies with him and Ruari in the kitchen. When she used to love him.

Bonnie took a bowl of melted chocolate, using it like a glue to adhere the walls together, then smoothed away any excess with a palette knife. She took out a canister and sprayed the area where she'd just worked.

'What's that, some sort of edible glue?' It looked like a can of spray paint, or something you'd use to oil a creaking joint. He'd hoped that though the sculpture was going to be primarily for show, it would still be edible.

Bonnie smiled. 'It's freeze spray to speed up the process, or else you'll be standing there all night waiting for that chocolate to set.'

She peeled his fingers away and they waited tentatively to see if the structure would hold fast. Sighing their relief when it did.

'Now we just need to do that about a hundred more times,' she said with a grin.

'Whatever it takes. Have you been working on this all day?' He wanted to gently broach the subject of footfall with her to get some idea of sales. If she'd been working mostly in the kitchen today, it suggested she hadn't been particularly troubled at the counter.

'In between sales. There's been a steady trickle of customers since the castle reopened. I think most people stop by, but there's no incentive for them to hang around and spend money, you know? I think we should at least start doing teas and coffees again. I've got all the equipment here, and if business picks up, we could look again at expanding into desserts et cetera. I'm not giving up.'

It was obvious in the set of her jaw that she was determined to put in whatever hours, and work, it took to make this viable. Ewen wasn't going to stand in her way, though he still had to be practical about things pertaining to his side of the business.

'Don't you need hygiene certificates and food-safety awareness before you do that?'

'All of which I have. I needed those even to come here. This was everything I wanted, so the moment I knew it was a possibility to run my own chocolate shop I did all the courses I needed.' Whatever she'd gone through prior to coming here, Bonnie had obviously channelled her strength into something positive. Making plans for her future. Something he had yet to do beyond his obligatory year in residence at BenCrag.

'I suppose we can start with the beverage side of the business and see how it goes from there. Am I done here?' She'd started adding the turrets now the walls were standing without his support, and, now he was satisfied she was going to produce something newsworthy on the day, he could rest easy.

'I can do the rest of the castle myself, thanks. However, I do have about two hundred raspberry and chocolate hearts to make for the wedding guests, if you'd like to assist me?' She pulled out the plastic moulds she was going to be using and set them on the counter in front of him.

Ewen knew to refuse help would seem churlish after promising to support her. It wasn't tiredness, or a lack of interest in the process, that made him hesitate. There was just something, a little warning light going off in his head every time he spent time with Bonnie, that told him to be careful.

Although he knew the end of his relationship with Victoria was best for him, he still missed having someone to share his life with. He didn't want to mistake that loneliness for something else.

With each revelation about Bonnie's courage, her work ethic, not to mention her company, he worried about getting too close to her. They both had baggage to deal with, and he certainly wasn't ready to get involved with anyone again. Not when he was emotionally battered from Victoria's betrayal, and having to relive the way his parents treated him at BenCrag after Ruari's death. The rejection and subsequent abandonment from people he loved, people who were supposed to love *him*, were too great to risk going through it all again with someone else.

Apart from anything else, he didn't know where he was going to be this time next year. Something he knew wasn't going to go down well with Bonnie when this place had been a lifeline for her. Before that happened, he was going to make sure there were provisions for her either here with the new owner, or somewhere more beneficial. Perhaps he could even get her started in her own premises in town. Whatever happened, he wasn't going to let her down the way she had been in the past. Starting with learning how to make raspberry chocolate hearts apparently…

Bonnie could tell he wasn't comfortable being the pupil in this scenario, but, since he'd offered his assistance, she wasn't going to send him away now. It was the only way she was going to get everything done in time without pulling an all-nighter. She'd lectured him on accepting help to achieve his goals, so it would be foolish not to take heed of her own advice. Especially when the stakes were so high.

Although the castle reopening under new ownership had drawn some interest, the already dwindling numbers suggested they couldn't sustain that novelty value for too long. She hoped that the summer holidays would provide more tourists, but they needed something to really pull in a crowd. Working on this showpiece was her way of highlighting her abilities, and making people aware of the shop's existence. Although she had been wondering if she'd bitten off more than she could chew until Ewen had showed up. Now the castle cast in chocolate was beginning to take shape, she was regaining her belief in herself.

Taking a leaf out of the book of other, similar businesses, she wondered if offering chocolate-making classes for children, or even a romantic couples evening of truffle-making, would increase interest and profits. The next initiative, once she proved to Ewen that she was capable of making teas and coffees. Her head was full of ideas and incentives, but he would need convincing that she could produce the goods. Further motivation to get this castle finished.

Ewen rolled up his sleeves as he awaited her instructions. Bonnie couldn't help but smile to herself, enjoying this little bit of temporary power. Tonight she was in charge, a complete role reversal for them both.

'I'll show you how to do the first couple, then you can do the rest. That'll free me up to finish the showpiece.'

Ewen nodded, his brow creased with concentration, obviously taking this more seriously than she'd expected.

'I hope I'll get credit for these when the time comes.'

'Certainly. Especially if they're not up to my standard.' She ignored Ewen's glare to retrieve the bowl of dried raspberries she'd put in the fridge earlier.

'Just show me what I need to do. How hard could it be?' The challenge was there in Ewen's mischievous blue eyes, but Bonnie wasn't going to rise to the baiting. She knew exactly how difficult it was to create something of a high enough standard befitting a wedding. Otherwise she wouldn't have spent the better part of a week perfecting her techniques before tackling this project. Ewen would find out for himself soon enough how much skill it took for something so simple.

And yes, she was running the risk of Ewen making a mess of the treats she'd planned for the wedding guests, and giving herself extra work fixing it all. It would be worth it though, just to see him sweat.

* * *

Ewen was sweating already. Bonnie, of course, remained cool as a cucumber as she toiled away on her architectural masterpiece. He'd sprinkled some dried raspberry into the circular moulds, and had now been tasked with tempering the chocolate, via the use of the microwave and a thermometer.

'You should check on that chocolate, Ewen,' she called over her shoulder. 'If you leave it in there too long it could crystallise and you'll have to start over again.'

He definitely didn't want that, when he was already feeling the pressure to get this right.

'Yes, boss.' He knew she liked him to call her that because it made her smile. And, because it made her smile, he'd been saying it frequently. He found himself wanting to please her.

This seemed to be her happy place, working in her chocolate shop, building something spectacular, and he wished he could promise it for ever.

'Check the temperature now,' she instructed as she removed the bowl of chocolate for him and replaced it with a bowl of white chocolate to be zapped.

Once the thermometer registered the required temperature, he checked with Bonnie before proceeding. 'Okay, I think that's it ready now.'

'So, you want to pour that into this thing that

looks like a funnel and decant the chocolate into the moulds, until it reaches just below the surface.' Bonnie demonstrated, carefully controlling the amount of melted chocolate dispensed using the lever on the side of the device, before handing it over to him.

Ewen took control, with Bonnie watching from over his shoulder, and squeezed the lever to release the flow of molten chocolate. Worried it was going to come out too fast, he let go, shutting off the steady stream. 'How's that?'

He could hear the grimace in her voice without looking at her. 'It's a little shy. We need them all consistent, so you can afford to add a little more.'

'Very diplomatic.' He dripped in an extra layer before moving on to the next one, taking his time to get it right. Too much time apparently.

'You need to speed up before the chocolate begins to set and it becomes harder to get out of the dispenser. It doesn't matter if it gets messy, we can tidy that up later.' When she moved to retrieve her own chocolate, Ewen took the opportunity to fill the rest of the tray without an audience, with some varying degrees of success.

'Not bad,' she noted, whilst stirring and testing her own batch, before putting it back in the microwave. Then she took the chocolate dispenser and topped up every single mould to the exact same level. It told of years of practice and expertise that he obviously didn't have, and never would.

'Okay, I admit it, this is harder than it looks.' He held his hands up and watched the smile of triumph cross over Bonnie's lips.

'And?'

'And you're the expert, not me. Clearly.'

As if to show him up even more, she took a spatula, drew it across the back of the mould in one swift move, cleaning away all the excess chocolate to leave perfectly shaped hearts. 'We'll leave those to set and you can get on with doing the rest.'

Ewen groaned, faced with the empty moulds laid out before him, and another bowl of chocolate ready to start the process all over again. Bonnie swirled some green food colouring in with her tempered white chocolate then set to work with a paintbrush, dabbing some moss onto the castle walls and the cliffs below. She truly was a master at work. Now everyone else would get to see it too.

Bonnie was enjoying herself. Now the castle was finally coming together, and Ewen was knocking out the heart-shaped chocolates, with her help, she wasn't feeling the pressure as much. Okay, so trade wasn't where she wanted it to be, but it would take time to build the business and her reputation, so she wasn't going to stress over it yet. Not when she was having so much fun watching Ewen eat humble pie.

Her stomach rumbled with the thought of food. The constant aroma of cocoa and vanilla often quelled her appetite, and she'd worked through lunch today to try and get her centrepiece finished. Ewen's help meant she had a little breathing room and had given her an appetite.

'Have you eaten? I might make an omelette if you'd like one?'

'Sure. Do you need me to get some stuff from the kitchen?'

'No need. I have some supplies here to keep me going through the day. There should be enough to make a couple of omelettes. Ham and mushroom okay for you?'

'Add some cheese and I'm yours for ever.'

Bonnie knew he was only joking, that they were only talking about food here, but Ewen's words sent a shiver along her skin. She grabbed her cardigan from the back of the chair and shrugged it on, refusing to believe the goosebumps could be attributed to anything other than the cool kitchen climate. Certainly not because she was thinking about Ewen's strong, thick forearms, and how it would feel to have them wrapped around her...

'Onion?' She tried to focus on the job at hand, and ended up shouting out randomly, earning her a bemused stare from Ewen.

'Yes, please,' he shouted back.

She turned on the extractor fan, more to cover her embarrassment than to diffuse the smell, and fumes, of her cooking. On autopilot, she diced up the ingredients and added them to the beaten eggs already cooking in the pan. A sprinkle of herbs, then she folded it over, before scooping it onto a plate and setting it in front of Ewen.

He was staring at her.

'Where's yours?'

'I'm going to make it now.' She gestured back at the ingredients spread out on the worktops ready for round two.

He was still staring at her.

'What?' She was worried now that she hadn't cooked it the way he wanted, or had made some sort of social faux pas. It was true, she hadn't cooked for anyone in a long time, so it was possible she'd done something wrong.

'You don't have to serve me, Bonnie. Sit down and eat your dinner first. In fact, I'm a grown man. I can make my own.' He seemed to get increasingly agitated, to the point where he got to his feet and pushed his chair back.

When he came towards Bonnie, she instinctively flinched, drawing a scowl from him in response.

'Sorry,' she squeaked, seeing the look on his face.

'You have nothing to apologise for. I just wanted you to sit down and enjoy your food.' Ewen pulled out the chair for her to sit on and took a step back, letting her reclaim her personal space.

Though Bonnie appreciated the gesture, she hated that he now felt the need to do it. To treat her as something fragile he needed to tiptoe around for fear of breaking her. She had only herself to blame. As usual. He wasn't aware that it was a reflex when a man came near her.

'Thanks.' She sat down, and, though her appetite had diminished, she stabbed the omelette with her fork. Damn her ex for still having the power to make her feel this way, cowed even by a man she'd battled with nearly every day since they'd met and who'd never once posed a threat to her. Flinching, in anticipation of a blow, was a reaction she didn't know if she'd ever grow out of. It also made her wonder if she'd ever let another man close to her, either as a friend or more. She hated that Ed continued to impact her life without even trying.

She swallowed down her bite of omelette along with the tears she was determined not to shed. Her ex didn't deserve any more of them.

Ewen turned away to make himself some dinner and she was grateful to him for not pushing her for an explanation of her behaviour. She wasn't ready to share the details of her life before BenCrag just yet, if ever. Perhaps being around him would help her realise that not all men acted the way Ed had. She felt more like herself around him. At least until just now, when she'd reverted momentarily to that submissive housewife role she'd been forced to assume for most of her adulthood.

She sawed into the rest of her omelette, forcing herself to finish it and deny Ed another victory. Okay, so he'd broken her, but that didn't mean she was fragile. She was still here, surviving without him, soon to thrive. Proving to him and everyone she wasn't a victim, but a warrior who would fight back with everything she had in her. It helped that Ewen could see that in her, even when he'd known her for only a short while. Letting her know that the old Bonnie was still a part of her.

'This is becoming something of a habit,' Ewen said, sitting down at the table opposite her with his burnt omelette offering.

'Pardon me?'

'Us. Having dinner together.' Ewen prodded his omelette, inspecting it before he dared to eat any of it.

'Well, it's weird pretending we're not ostensibly living together. I don't suppose it hurts to have some company every now and again.' Especially if she was going to freak out every time she was alone with a man. At least socialising with Ewen might go some way to helping her learn to trust again.

'Don't flatter me too much.' He feigned offence, but Bonnie could tell he wasn't too bothered.

Although he'd been spiky when they first met, often stressed over the happenings at the castle, he didn't strike her as someone who would go out of his way to hurt anyone. So far tonight Ewen had been nothing but considerate of her feelings, and her emotional hang-ups, despite not knowing all the details. The hallmarks of a good man.

'As if I would,' she sparked back, and moved to the sink to deposit her dirty dishes.

When she felt him moving behind her to leave his now empty plate in the sink too, she tensed, though did her best not to react the way she had earlier.

'I don't know what happened to you in the past, Bonnie, but I would never hurt you,' he said softly, his kindness undoing her so that tension in her body melted away.

She turned around to face him. 'I know.'

The small space between them was suddenly

filled with an air of expectation and anticipation. A feeling that something was about to happen.

'Would it be okay if I gave you a hug?' he asked, though he didn't move.

'I'd like that.' She loved that he was asking permission to even comfort her. Understanding that she needed to take control of who touched her body, how, and why, without knowing anything of her circumstances. Realising that right now a hug was a huge step for her. As was trusting a man to touch her without expecting anything in return or lashing out if she didn't acquiesce to his needs.

Ewen wouldn't take offence if she walked away right now, seeking sanctuary alone in her room. Except an unconditional hug was everything she'd needed for such a long time.

When he opened his arms wide, she went willingly to him. Let him wrap her up in his strong embrace and hold her close to his solid chest.

'You're safe here, Bonnie.'

It wasn't clear if he meant safe in the castle, or in his arms, but she knew she wanted to remain in both for the foreseeable future.

CHAPTER FIVE

'HAVE YOU SEEN the bride?' Ewen sidled up to Bonnie and whispered into her ear.

Since letting him hold her two nights ago in the kitchen, she'd learned to enjoy the warmth of his body near her, rather than fear it. Even if the moments after had proved a little awkward. She'd thanked him for his help with the chocolate making, before retiring back to her room out of harm's way. Where she'd had to deal with the new emotions he'd brought to the fore.

It wasn't just that it was a new experience to have someone show her so much compassion, there was something more beneath that solace he provided. She liked him. Yes, he was handsome, as illustrated by the Harris tartan kilt and jacket he was wearing today. But there was also a bond forming between them, despite their obvious differences. He was wealthy, upper class, whilst she was broke and essentially homeless without his assistance. Yet there was a vulnerability she recognised in him. He'd been hurt too. Not physically perhaps, but he was nonetheless scarred. They were both battle weary, yet it seemed as though they'd begun to open up to one another. Ewen was making her transition back into the real world a little easier. And had she mentioned how hot he was in the formal outfit he'd begrudgingly put on for the wedding today?

'Earth to Bonnie. Did you hear me? The bride has apparently gone AWOL. That wedding planner is going nuts outside.' The concern in Ewen's voice drew Bonnie's attention away from his thick, hairy legs to the real reason she was standing here at the entrance to the function room.

She'd only come to watch the ceremony from a distance, not play a part, except that of chocolatier. Unlike Ewen, who was playing genial host, she was background staff only. So she didn't know why he was coming to her now with this news.

'I'm sure she'll turn up. The bridal car has probably just been held up somewhere.' With the money that had been spent on this event, there was no doubt in Bonnie's mind that it would be going ahead.

'The car is already here. The bridesmaids said she went to the bathroom when they got here and disappeared. What am I going to do, Bonnie?' The panic was evident in his voice and his wide eyes.

She wanted to tell him it wasn't her problem, hell, it wasn't even his problem. However, he'd dug her out of a hole on two occasions now. It was also important to both of them that today went well. The least she could do was help him look for their runaway bride.

'Okay. I'll check the ladies' bathroom, then meet you out front in the garden.'

Ewen nodded at the suggestion, probably glad for something productive to do rather than letting pure panic set in. There was a room full of expectant wedding guests, a groom sweating at the end of the aisle, and a bewildered registrar constantly checking his watch, probably because he had another ceremony to go to after this one. At least the pianist, who'd been drafted in along with his very expensive piano just for the occasion, was managing to entertain the waiting congregation with a selection of popular show tunes in the meantime.

'Janey? Are you in there?' Bonnie ducked her head into the bathroom and called out, but there was no one inside. The halls of the castle appeared to be littered with worried bridesmaids tottering on impossible heels, attached to their phones.

Assuming by the hysterical voices that the blushing bride hadn't come out of hiding, Bonnie left the band of cerise-silk-clad worrywarts behind and headed outside. Ewen had wandered down by the beautiful wisteria-covered pergola. The sun shining through the lilac blossoms created a fiery red halo effect around his head. He looked quite the romantic lead and could almost have passed for the groom himself. Though she was sure he wasn't any more interested in getting married than she was. Bonnie suspected it would take a great deal of trust for either of them ever to enter into a long-term commitment like that again.

'Any joy?' he asked as she made her way over to him.

She shook her head and watched the hope die in his eyes. 'If she's changed her mind, shouldn't we leave her be? Clearly she doesn't want to be found.'

This was apparently more than a bride having a bathroom break. If Janey had seen some last-minute red flags and decided not to tie herself to this man for the rest of her life, Bonnie wanted to respect that.

'It does suggest that she's upset and I wouldn't want to leave her out here alone.'

Damn it, he was so logical sometimes, as well as considerate.

'Okay, I'll help look for her, but I want you to promise we're not going to force her to go back there. I don't want her to feel under pressure to do something she doesn't want to.'

'I totally understand. I just want to make sure she's all right. Cross my heart.' He made the action of the cross on the left side of his chest. That was enough to convince Bonnie they weren't going to be complicit in aiding another toxic relationship.

'Well, if it was me running away from my groom and a room full of people, I wouldn't be standing under this photo-op pergola in full view. I think we should look somewhere a little more inconspicuous. You know this place better than I do—any suggestions?' They were a tad isolated up here on the cliffs. A bride in a full wedding dress would have been noticeable running down the driveway, so she imagined Janey had retreated into the trees, seeking shelter like a lost lamb.

In a way that was probably what she was. There'd been plenty of times when Bonnie had felt alone, not knowing where she was going, or how to get out of the situation she was in. Ewen was right. She needed someone to reassure her, and, if necessary, book her a taxi out of here as soon as possible.

'There are a few hidden gems further back in the trees where we used to hide out when we were kids.' It wasn't more than a brief mention of his brother, but Bonnie knew it was bound to cause him pain. Whilst that wasn't something she could assist him with, she was able to help him in his current quest.

'Lead the way.' She hung back and let him forge a path down to the trees along the estate boundary, following behind and wishing she hadn't worn heels.

Away from the expertly trimmed lawns, and carefully tended gardens around the castle, the surrounding woods were a wild tangle of trees and brush. It would have been a haven for two young brothers to explore. Bonnie wasn't sure how well it suited a bride in a full meringue gown when even she was in danger of having her modest, not at all poofy, strappy floral sundress torn to shreds. Ewen, on the other hand, was striding through briar and bramble in his kilt, looking every inch a true highlander. He had such a capable strength about him that she couldn't imagine him ever being hurt by anything, yet someone had clearly wounded him deeply. It made her wonder if that tough exterior was the armour he chose to wear now to prevent further injury, and what he'd been like before all of the heartache.

Not that it mattered to her, when he was still the man who'd held her in his arms, given her a job and a place to stay. The person he was now was everything she needed. She just wished he'd never had to go through the things he had to get here.

'We used to have a den down here made out of broken branches and bits of old fencing. It was nothing more than a lean-to, really, that would have collapsed on top of us with little effort. But it was special. It was ours, you know?' He stopped long enough to give her a hangdog look that said he missed those simple, carefree days.

Bonnie didn't remember having any of those. Even as a child she'd had her father telling her what to do, spending her spare time working in the shop, which had felt like a punishment then. Now she was grateful for the skills she'd learned in his chocolate shop. She was glad Ewen had some happier memories to look back on.

'Did you come down here a lot?' She was sure life in a castle had been much different from growing up above a chocolate shop, but things were never as much fun as they appeared from the outside. Her friends used to be jealous of her easy access to the sweet stuff, and yes, she had purloined some of the stock to buy friends with at times, but life at home had always been hard work.

'Whenever we could. We'd take food from the kitchen and bring our comics down here to read. All Ruari's doing, of course. Believe it or not, he was the troublemaker, leading me astray.' His lopsided smile told of how close he'd been to his brother, and just how much he missed him.

Bonnie wanted nothing more in that moment than to offer him comfort, but she knew from experience coming into close contact with him wasn't something easily forgotten. A hug wasn't just a hug when she never wanted to leave his embrace. A frightening revelation for her when she needed to assert her independence, and not throw her lot in with another man.

'I'm not going back.' A voice sounded somewhere from the trees, interrupting Bonnie and Ewen's heart-to-heart before she did something she might regret. Bonnie was grateful for it.

'Janey?' It took a moment before Bonnie realised where the voice had come from. Then the bride appeared, resplendent in white lace and satin, from an old arbour hidden in the thicket.

Janey hitched up the train of her dress as though she was getting ready to run again.

Ewen held up a hand to appease her. 'We're just here to make sure you're all right.'

'You don't have to do anything you don't want to, Janey, but you can't stay out here for ever.' There would come a time when she would have to face up to her situation and make a decision about her future. Bonnie just hoped she didn't take as long as she had.

'I know. I'm sorry if I've spoiled the day. I suppose everyone's waiting for me back there.' Janey sat down on the wrought-iron seat that had been hidden from Bonnie's view by the ivy-covered trellis around it.

She took a seat beside the anxious bride and took her hand. 'Don't worry about anyone else. If you've decided you don't want to go through with this, I'm sure we can get a car to take you some place away from the madness.'

Bonnie looked to Ewen, who nodded. 'I have my car. Just give me the word and I'll take you anywhere you want to go.'

'I just need a minute to think things through and make sure this is really what I want,' Janey explained, and Ewen and Bonnie both fell silent.

Except a million thoughts were running through Bonnie's head that she could never live with herself if she didn't voice out loud. It mightn't make any difference, just as her parents' opinions hadn't mattered to her before she'd committed to the wrong man, but Bonnie thought it worth trying.

'Has Lawrence done anything to…to hurt you?' She knew it was a difficult subject to tackle, but one she couldn't in good conscience shy away from.

Janey stared at her. 'You mean like cheated, or anything? No. He's very loyal.'

'No… I mean has he ever…physically hurt you, or tried to tell you what to do, how to behave?' She could feel Ewen's eyes burning into her, looking for answers as to why she should ask such a question. Though she hadn't intended on sharing details of her past with anyone, it was more important to save Janey from making the same mistakes she had.

There were always warning signs of a potentially controlling partner, even if that blinding love often masked the problems at first. In hindsight, her ex was always calling, checking in with her, seeing who she was with and what she was doing. Young and naïve, she'd liked the attention, believing it was his way of showing how much he cared. That he was always thinking about her. She hadn't seen him gradually exerting control over her until it was too late and she had nowhere else to go.

Ewen coughed discreetly, his subtle way of telling her not to interfere. Perhaps even that she was crossing a line, but she didn't know where she would've ended up if she'd actually married her ex. If Janey was having doubts now, it didn't bode well for the future.

'What? No?' Janey was frowning at her, obviously outraged.

Bonnie blushed, aware that she'd projected her own issues onto the woman. Though she sup-

posed it was good news that Lawrence wasn't
a potentially abusive scumbag. 'Sorry. I just
wanted to check that this wasn't a cry for help.'

'I didn't ask for help. I came here for some
time alone. Lawrence is a kind, loving man I
am lucky to be marrying.' In a fit of pique, she
gathered up her skirts and stomped off out of
the woods, leaving Ewen and Bonnie staring at
one another.

Ewen couldn't keep the look of concern from
his face. 'Are you okay?'

'What? Yes. I'm fine,' Bonnie huffed, embarrassed that he'd witnessed her epic fail, revealing way too much of her own issues in trying
to help the bride. It appeared she still had a long
way to go with her own healing, as well as her
social skills.

'Bonnie, I get the impression that something
happened before you came to BenCrag. Do you
want to talk about it?'

'No. The bride's gone back to her groom,
that's all that matters.' Her eyes were prickling
with tears because of the memories she'd conjured, all in vain apparently. It was clear she
hadn't left the past entirely behind after all. Especially when Ewen could tell she was keeping
some sort of big dark secret to herself. Bonnie
didn't want him to know she'd been weak and
let someone take advantage of her to the de-

gree that Ed had, but clearly keeping it to herself hadn't worked.

In an effort to retain some of her dignity, Bonnie attempted to flounce off too. Only to stick her foot straight into the end of a log lying in her path. She found herself falling forward, feeling as though it were happening in slow motion as she did her best to maintain her balance, though she knew the end was inevitable. Her dignified exit was going to end up with her face first in the dirt. With Ewen there to watch her further humiliation.

Except, before she got a face full of moss and twigs, a strong pair of arms grabbed her around the waist from behind and pulled her back upright. Ewen knocked the wind out of her as she hit his chest with a thump.

'Sorry. Did I hurt you?'

'No. I, er…you've got quick reflexes.' She blurted out the second thing that came into her head. Glad she didn't voice the first. Otherwise Ewen would know how much she liked the intimate feel of him against her. Although her almost purr might have given it away…

'I wouldn't want you to turn up to your big event with mud on your face.'

Maybe she was imagining it, but she thought Ewen's voice was deeper than usual as he spoke directly into her ear. She definitely wasn't flinching any more when he came close to her. If anything, her body was responding to him in a way she hadn't felt in a long time. Being around him had made her realise not all men were to be feared, and that had let other sensations take over. Excitement. That the awareness of a solid male body could awaken more than terror inside her. *Desire.* Something she didn't know if she was ready to explore again, and certainly not with her boss.

He eventually let go of his hold on her and she brushed herself down. Wiping away the feel of him against her, and all of those emotions she wasn't ready to deal with yet.

'My big event…' She gave a fake laugh. 'I'm not the one getting married.'

'No, but it's a new chapter in your life too. I know you'll want to look your best.' He gave her a smile and Bonnie could see he genuinely cared. Ewen seemed to understand what she needed, and when. Always there to catch her and put her back on her feet. If she wasn't careful, she'd come to rely on him, and that was when the trouble would really start.

'You can talk to me, Bonnie.' Ewen didn't want to let the matter drop. He could tell she'd been through something traumatic and wanted to help. There'd been certain comments that had raised his suspicions about her ex, added to the circumstances of her arrival when she'd come to BenCrag homeless and broke. Then there was the way she'd flinched in the kitchen when he'd come near her. He'd held back from asking at the time, wanting only to reassure her he wasn't a threat, to support her and offer the hug they'd both needed.

Now, hearing her counsel someone else about the dangers of an abusive partner, things were beginning to add up to an unpalatable scenario. He could no longer hold his tongue, and wanted her to know he was there for her.

Though their relationship had been antagonistic at the start, they were clearly two lonely, wounded people. He knew what it was like to suffer emotionally, with no family or friends around to turn to. It was human nature to want to help Bonnie and he tried not to read any more than that into it.

'About what?' She blinked at him, feigning an ignorance that didn't suit her.

Ewen narrowed his eyes. 'You. Your ex. It doesn't take a genius to work out something seriously bad happened there. I just want you to know I'm here if you want to talk about it.'

Bonnie stared at him, her eyes filling with tears and something that looked very like fear. He swore and wrapped his arms around her in a hug. Despite her defensive nature, there was something about her that made him want to protect her, now more than ever. As though he knew she was just as vulnerable inside as he was.

Only when her face was buried in his chest did she deign to speak. 'I let Ed control me for ten years. Who I spoke to. What I wore. Everything. And it still wasn't enough to make him happy.'

'Did he hurt you?' Ewen's jaw tightened even as he said the words. He hated to think of any man thinking it was okay to raise a hand to a woman, but to imagine Bonnie cowering in terror under the threat of violence made his blood boil.

She was such a feisty spirit, the level of control it would have taken to make her submit to someone else's will was unimaginable.

He felt her nod against him and his heart broke into a thousand pieces for her.

'I'm so sorry. Is there anything I can do?' It seemed like such a clichéd thing to say, but he felt powerless in the circumstances. He wanted to make things better for her, to take away the pain, all the while knowing it was impossible.

Bonnie pried herself away from his body, and, though he wanted to keep her safe in his embrace for ever, getting her to open up was a huge step. One she likely needed to take so she could begin to heal.

'He's in prison. The women who took me in at the refuge persuaded me to report him to the police. So he won't be free for some time. There's no need to turn vigilante on my account.' She gave him a half-hearted smile, which did little to persuade him she was okay. For her abuser to end up in prison suggested it had been a serious assault. Something Bonnie did not deserve under any circumstances.

'I'm so sorry you had to go through all of that, and for how I treated you on your arrival here. I can only say I'd just gone through a break-up too. Nothing as serious as yours, of course, but I was licking my wounds when you turned up, and not in the mood for company. You deserved better and I'm sorry.'

He understood now why she'd been so combative at the time. She'd been fighting to keep hold of the new start that had been promised to her, trying to leave all the bad stuff that had happened behind. Yet instead of providing support, he'd done everything to try and get rid of her. Adding to her stress because he'd wanted to wallow alone.

'It's not your fault. I guess we were both a bit tender at the time. So, did your partner not want to become lady of the manor, then?' Bonnie was angling for some information and it would be churlish of him not to share after she'd poured her heart out to him. Even if it was embarrassing to admit he hadn't been good enough for Victoria.

'She never got the opportunity. By the time I'd heard about my father, Victoria had already found someone with a bigger bank account and title. I think I was just a placeholder until someone better came along.'

'Well, I'm sure she's kicking herself now.' Bonnie offered him a bright smile that was much nicer to see on her face than the pain of reliving her recent troubles. The one positive to come out of his humiliating love life.

'I don't know about that, but I do believe we weren't right for each other.' In hindsight, he'd always been holding a part of himself back. He'd been hurt so much by his parents' rejection he'd been afraid to give his heart completely. The only part of Ewen Harris Victoria had really known was the successful businessman. He hadn't shared anything of his family life, or the strained relationship he'd had with his parents. Bonnie hadn't been here long and she knew more about him than Victoria ever had, illustrating the fact that he'd never felt comfortable enough around her to just be himself. Perhaps he'd been so keen to fill the void left by his family that he'd clung onto the relationship even when it clearly hadn't been working. It had taken being around Bonnie to understand that.

Victoria wouldn't have settled for takeaway in front of the telly, or chased runaway brides with him. And he certainly had never felt able to open up emotionally to her. The split was probably a blessing in disguise, it had simply taken him this long to see that. Now all he had to worry about was what this bond between him and Bonnie meant for the future he'd planned away from the castle.

'You did a good job with Janey,' Ewen whispered as the happy couple took their seats at the top table. After the short delay, and with the congregation none the wiser about the bride's emotional breakdown in the garden, or their hosts' heart-to-heart, Janey and Lawrence had exchanged their vows and joined together in holy matrimony.

Bonnie narrowed her eyes at him, as though she was waiting for the punchline, but she'd been brave in asking the questions she had. It had focused Janey on the important things too, helping her realise she had a good man, and it was just wedding-day jitters after all. Hearing of her experiences had also given him a better insight into the woman he was working with. Given him more reason to admire her, even though his head was telling him to fight against it.

'I'm serious. They look happy.' He supposed he was envious of that, though both he and Bonnie had reason to be sceptical about romance when they'd been conned by it in the past.

'I'm pleased for them.'

Now it was Ewen's turn to look sceptical.

Bonnie nudged him with her elbow. 'Hey, I'm sure it works for some people. And if you're going to be vying for wedding venue of the year, then you need to start playing the role of host with a little more enthusiasm.'

'You want me to start weeping tears of joy? I'm afraid I'm not the sentimental type.' Finding out about Victoria's betrayal had made him cynical about the whole idea of marriage.

Once upon a time he'd imagined they'd get married, have children, and be a family. Something he hadn't been part of for a long time. Looking back, he could see she wasn't the type of woman who would've been content with the vision he had for two-point-four children and a Labrador. Victoria enjoyed the party lifestyle too much to give it up for cosy nights in, and she'd never professed otherwise. Ewen had been the one who'd pretended to be someone he wasn't to impress her. Splurging on luxury holidays abroad, partying with the rich and famous, when all he really wanted was someone to settle down with. Now he'd had some time and space to see things more clearly, he realised Victoria hadn't been entirely to blame for the breakdown in their relationship. She might have cheated on him, but he hadn't been honest with her about who he was, or what he wanted. The family he'd been missing for so long.

Now he didn't think he'd ever let anyone close enough to even think of marriage again. He could only imagine the pain he'd endure if he married someone, shared his life with them, and they later cheated on him. Once was enough. Further proof that he wasn't worthy of love, on top of his parents' rejection. Well, he didn't intend to put himself through any more heartache. Single life seemed the way to go if he was ever going to have peace.

'I don't believe that for a second. Otherwise you wouldn't be doing this in the first place.' Bonnie reminded him that hosting this wedding hadn't been a foregone conclusion. He would've been within his rights as the new owner, not to mention a grieving son, to cancel the booking. Fulfilling the obligation had been more about honouring his father's wishes than appeasing the couple making a lifetime commitment to one another.

Perhaps he and his parents hadn't had much of a relationship in Ewen's adult years, but he had hoped, by honouring his father's commitments, he would find some sort of closure. So far, it remained elusive.

'Well, I guess I can only try to hold it together. Looks like it's showtime.' As the guests babbled excitedly at the table, waiting for the speeches to begin, Ewen knew it was expected of him to say a few words first.

His hands were sweating as he walked up to take the mic, even though he was used to speaking in public. Setting up his own business, and subsequently selling it, had meant having to be vocal, able to sell himself. After leaving home he'd had to do everything himself, and he'd learned to control his nerves in this kind of situation. But championing newly-weds was definitely out of his comfort zone given his recent history.

He felt Bonnie's hand on his back. 'Go get 'em, tiger.'

It put a smile on his face, and a want to forget all the other people in the room and stay with her. Every time they touched he was reminded he had an ally, that he was no longer on his own. It didn't matter that Bonnie was technically an employee, only here due to the fact she had nowhere else to go, because they had a connection beyond that. Despite all his intentions otherwise, he had let someone in. He'd only known Bonnie a matter of days, yet he felt more comfortable talking about his feelings with her than someone he'd lived with for years. It was both refreshing, and terrifying.

And that was before he even tackled the way she made him feel. Beyond his admiration, and the kinship, that she evoked in him, there was something more primal awakening inside him. A want to protect her from any more harm, but also a desire he knew he could never follow up on. That night in the kitchen he'd enjoyed having her in his arms, her soft warmth pressed against him. Today, catching her in the woods, he'd wanted the same again. He'd resisted not only because it would complicate things when they were working and living together, but also because he didn't think Bonnie would welcome it. Although she'd gone willingly to him for comfort once, it didn't mean she was ready for anything more. He knew he wasn't either.

Never mind that he wasn't prepared to risk his heart on anyone again, he also didn't have any intention of sticking around longer than necessary. After everything she'd been through, Bonnie wasn't the kind of woman who could be picked up and dropped at will. She deserved more. Nothing good could come out of acting on whatever these growing feelings for her were. Experience had told him that getting close to anyone only ended in heartbreak for him. The best he could hope was that these feelings would gradually fade away and save them both the pain that seemed to come with emotional attachment. For him at least.

For the time being, romance had to be reserved for paying customers at the castle only.

Ewen took the microphone and addressed the assembled guests, his eyes firmly on Bonnie at the back of the room to keep him grounded. 'Good afternoon, everyone. I'm the owner of BenCrag Castle, the current Duke of Arbay, and I'd like to thank you all for joining us to congratulate the marriage of Lawrence and Janey.'

He started a round of applause and turned to give a nod to the couple of the moment, continuing his speech once the clapping finished. 'I just want to wish you both the very best for the future. Love doesn't come around for everyone, and you're very lucky to have found it with each other. Thank you for sharing your big day with us at the castle, and as a gift from us to you, to mark the occasion, we have a special treat. Our resident chocolatier, Bonnie Abernathy, has created an entirely edible scale model of the castle for you.'

Bonnie took her cue and unveiled her chocolate masterpiece with a nervous smile. As he'd hoped, the reveal was met with a chorus of oohs and wows, along with a loud round of applause.

'We also have raspberry chocolate hearts for

everyone, made by our very own duke.' She clapped and directed attention back to him.

'I'd like to raise a glass and toast our happy couple before I hand you over for the speeches. To the bride and groom.' Ewen helped himself to a glass of champagne from a tray nearby and lifted it into the air, the rest of the guests joining in. He was glad when he was finally able to hand over the microphone to the wedding party, and jog back to Bonnie.

'Good job.' She patted him on the back as though he'd been the one who'd been slaving away for days, rather than someone who'd simply microwaved a bowl of chocolate and poured it into moulds.

'Hey, I did the easy part. Everyone can see where the real work was. Fingers crossed it leads to extra business for us both.' In these days of social media, and the obsession with photographing everything, Ewen hoped the guests would share images of the day far and wide.

'I've left some business cards on the table beside the chocolates. Maybe next time we should open the shop, or set up a stall in the hall for passing trade.'

Ewen knew she was joking, but he loved Bonnie's entrepreneurial spirit. It showed her ambition for the future. One he was sure he wouldn't be around to be a part of, and suddenly he was having second thoughts about his own plans.

'Ugh. You mean we have to do this all over again? You want to go to the bar? I think I need a drink.' Anything to blot out thoughts about the tasks he had ahead, and how much Bonnie was going to hate him in a year's time. He wanted to enjoy her company whilst he still had it.

CHAPTER SIX

'THANK GOODNESS THAT'S OVER.' Bonnie sat down opposite Ewen with a glass of white wine and kicked off her shoes. It was the first time they'd had a chance to really relax. With the bride and groom off to start their honeymoon, and taxis steadily arriving for the rest of the guests, the pressure was off.

Of course she could have left once she'd delivered her part of the deal, but Ewen had seemed as though he could use the backup. Once the formalities were over, and drink had been consumed, he'd been besieged by guests all wanting selfies with the handsome, kilted duke. She'd had her fair share of attention too with people congratulating her on her work and making enquiries about other custom creations. A sideline she would have to run by Ewen if anything came to fruition. The day had been a lot for two people who'd been rattling around the castle on their own for some time.

'Thanks for sticking around. I appreciate it.'

Ewen held up his whisky and clinked his glass to hers.

'Where else would I be? I mean, the sound in this place really travels so I may as well be here, watching you schmooze your fan club.' Bonnie was poking fun at the attention he'd received, mostly from the female members of the wedding party, but she could hear the tinge of bitterness in her voice.

Seeing him smiling and posing with his arm around random, glamorous women had woken something inside her. Something green, territorial, and beating its chest with rage. She didn't want to see him touching anyone else. Perhaps that was part of the reason she'd stayed on. To scare off potential suitors. Okay, and she also wouldn't be able to rest in another part of the castle thinking he was here partying with everyone else, without her. It was clear she was becoming closer to Ewen than she'd been prepared for, and she didn't know what to do about it.

'Hi. I really wanted to say what an amazing job you did of the chocolate. The raspberry hearts were amazing.' A young blonde, wearing a short turquoise strapless dress and a phenomenal amount of fake tan, approached their table.

'Thank you, but it was Ewen who made those...' Bonnie trailed off when she realised the woman wasn't even looking at her, her eyes locked onto her companion.

'They were yummy.' The blonde's now husky voice didn't sound as though she was still talking about the chocolates. Especially with that look in her eyes that said she was ready to devour Ewen, whether Bonnie was there or not.

'Feel free to drop into the shop to buy more any time. Bonnie has a wide variety of flavours in store.' Bless Ewen, he was doing his best to big up her shop, when it was clear Blondie had no interest in anything but him.

Bonnie didn't think he could be oblivious to the woman's interest. She wondered if he was just being polite, or if he didn't want to make a play for her in front of Bonnie. Either way she wasn't going to stick around to watch. She drained her glass and got up to leave.

'Can you take a pic of me and the duke?' Ewen's admirer thrust her phone at Bonnie and proceeded to sit in his lap. He didn't do anything to dissuade her.

Bonnie snapped a couple of pics then tossed the phone back at her. 'Here. I'll leave you two to it.'

She walked away, jaw clenched, hackles rising, and confused about why. Ewen wasn't hers, and she wasn't in any position to claim him even if he wanted her. He was the first man she'd really had contact with since leaving her ex. The only one she'd had any interest in. It terrified her that she was even thinking about opening her heart up to someone else when she was hurting already simply by being in the same room as him.

She didn't want to have these feelings for her boss and landlord, who already had more control over her life than she was comfortable with. If she lost herself to him, and things didn't work out, she would lose everything again. A relationship simply wasn't possible when there was so much at stake. Especially so soon after she'd left the last one. Her life at BenCrag was supposed to be a new start, her time to find herself again, and she wouldn't do that if she was mooning over someone she couldn't, and shouldn't, have. She only wished she could walk away from her feelings as easily as the scene at the bar.

She was about to climb the marble stairway up to her room when someone grabbed her arm. Ewen.

'Where are you going?'

'Bed.'

'Oh…did I do something to upset you? I thought we were having a nice time.' He looked genuinely puzzled as to why she'd want to leave.

'No offence, but I didn't want to be a gooseberry. You looked as though you were having a better time with your new friend.'

A slow smile across Ewen's lips. 'Wait…are you jealous?'

Bonnie shrugged his hand off her arm, not wanting him to touch her when she needed to be mad at him, instead of enjoying the contact.

She spat out a laugh. 'As if. It's nothing to do with me if you like having women drape themselves over you for attention.'

His smile grew broader until he was flashing his even white teeth, clearly enjoying tormenting her. 'You are. You're actually jealous.'

Bonnie couldn't even deny it when it was so obvious. So she gave him an eye roll and an exasperated tut, before attempting to walk away again.

'Wait. I'm sorry. I was only teasing. I didn't mean to be rude and leave you feeling like a spare part. I'm just not used to this. I've never really had to play up the whole family-connection thing before. It's a novelty for people. I don't take it too seriously. You shouldn't either.'

Bonnie didn't want him to be upset when he'd been having a good day. A rare thing for both of them, she suspected.

'When we first met I saw you as more of a Viking lumberjack. All outdoorsy and intimidating. Now I know you're really a homebody who likes takeaway in front of the TV.' Somebody she felt comfortable with, who made her feel as though she wasn't alone any more.

'Shh!' Ewen put his finger to her lips. 'That doesn't make me sound very glamorous.'

Despite the teasing tone, the energy between them had become something altogether more serious. He was standing so close, his finger was practically the only thing between their lips. She was very tempted to push it out of the way. Instead, she put a step even farther over that line.

'It's all I need.' She held eye contact with him, saw the darkening of his pupils, the tic in his jaw as he clenched his teeth together. There was a power in knowing, seeing, that she affected him just as much as he did her.

Her gaze fell to his mouth. She wanted to feel his lips hard and insistent on hers. His beard grazing her skin, turning her insides to mush in the process. It was nice to feel something other than fear being this close to a man again. Even if it still represented a danger of sorts. Though, in that moment, she didn't care about the repercussions of straying beyond the boundaries of their working relationship. All that mattered was the notion that he was about to kiss her.

'Your Grace, the last of the guests are leaving. Do you need me to stay on?'

Their moment was interrupted by the arrival of the housekeeper, who was either oblivious to their current situation, or too discreet to make a big deal out of it. She stood patiently waiting for a response as Bonnie and Ewen scrambled to regain their personal space from one another. The sudden separation and change of mood left her head spinning. Ewen, too, seemed flustered, not at all his usual confident self.

'Mrs McKenzie…we were just, er, discussing the, er—'

'We'll tidy up. You go on home.' Bonnie couldn't bear to watch him try to come up with an excuse and jumped in. Then realised that she didn't have any authority to say any such thing. 'That's if it's all right with you, Your Grace?'

'Yes. Of course. That's just what we were discussing, Mrs McKenzie. You've done so much already, it wouldn't be fair to expect you to stay any later.' Ewen was a bad liar, stumbling through his explanation so much Bonnie couldn't help but smile.

She liked that manipulating the truth to suit himself didn't come easily. It wasn't likely he did it on a regular basis when he was rambling so much just to cover up the fact they'd almost kissed. It was reassuring after being with a man who drove her crazy twisting her words until she hardly recognised the truth. She didn't imagine he was someone who felt the need to exert control over her, or anyone else, with lies. Or his fists. In any other circumstances Ewen would seem like the perfect man, but it was difficult to

get past the fact he held all the cards in the relationship they already had. To throw her heart
into the ring along with her financial stability
would be madness.

Even Mrs McKenzie could see through his
poor attempt at an excuse, folding her arms
with a sigh, eyeing Bonnie with some suspicion.
Goodness knew what she'd seen at the castle
over the years when this little interaction didn't
raise any more than an eyebrow.

'The caterers are packing away their dishes
now, so there shouldn't be too much mess left.'
She took her leave, only to turn back a second
later. 'Oh, and any more thoughts on the annual
ball, sir?'

Ewen grimaced. 'I'll get back to you on that,
and yes, I'll take another look for that address
book. Goodnight, Mrs McKenzie.'

'Goodnight.'

'So I guess I'm not going to bed, then?' Bonnie resigned herself to the fact she'd be spending the rest of the night cleaning up the mess
left behind by the inebriated wedding guests,
and nothing more exciting.

Even if she and Ewen had decided to lose their
minds and act on the attraction brewing between
them, Mrs McKenzie's interruption had given
her an opportunity to think things through more
clearly. The moment had passed now she remem-

bered they still had to live and work together. She wasn't ready for a relationship with anyone, least of all her boss. Nor was she the sort of person to go for one-night stands. Especially when they'd have to see each other every day at work. Giving into temptation now would only make things awkward between them in the future. She didn't want that, not when she'd found someone who made her feel safe for the first time in years.

'I'm sorry if you felt pressured into volunteering for clean-up duty.' Ewen walked back down the stairs with Bonnie, watching as the last of the staff, including Mrs McKenzie, left the building.

'It's okay. What else would I be doing anyway?' Other than perhaps making the second biggest mistake of her life, sleeping with her boss, and ruining the best thing to happen to her in a long time. She was trying not to think about the pros of that scenario, and how they might be working up a sweat under more exciting conditions.

He locked the doors, leaving them alone for the first time that day. Bonnie didn't want to wait around for that lightning to strike again. They mightn't escape it a second time, and ran the risk of getting frazzled in the process.

She walked into the function room which looked as though a tornado had swept through. Although the caterers had cleared away the dirty glasses and dishes, there were still empty bottles, food mess, and even confetti, littering the tables and floor.

'I'll get a broom.' Ewen disappeared, presumably to raid the cleaning supplies Mrs McKenzie kept locked away.

Bonnie busied herself clearing away the rubbish using the bin bags she found behind the makeshift bar that had been set up for the day. Separating the recyclable items from the rest to make it easier to dispose of.

'Who said life with you wasn't glamorous?' she said, scooping a pile of mashed potato off the table and dumping it into the rubbish bag.

'I did try to warn you it wasn't all champagne and waltzes around the salon floor. Sometimes you have to get your hands dirty too.' He scrunched his nose up as he picked up a single dirty sock between his thumb and forefinger and deposited it into the makeshift bin.

Bonnie's mind boggled as to how anyone had lost it without noticing, and what the circumstances for taking it off had been. She supposed a long day combined with alcohol consumption led to some dodgy decision-making. After all, she'd just been caught about to kiss her boss by another member of staff. Hopefully the trusted housekeeper could be relied upon for her discretion. It would be soul-destroying to lose everything now over a stupid crush. So Ewen was attractive. There was no point denying that when he'd had most of the people here today drooling over him. He was also the only man to have shown her any consideration in her entire life. Little wonder then that she'd confused that for something more.

Naturally her emotions were all over the place after being put through the wringer with Ed, who'd made her think she was going crazy by manipulating her feelings. If she didn't want to ruin the new life she'd set up for herself here at the castle, she needed to get a handle on these emotions, and keep her relationship with Ewen strictly professional.

'So what is this ball I've heard mention of? That sounds more in keeping with my idea of castle life. Do we wear gowns and waltz around the salon floor at that one?' Despite all the joking around, Bonnie had to admit the idea held some appeal for her. She couldn't remember the last time she'd had a chance to dress up and have fun. Today didn't count when they'd had to put in so much work and were currently reduced to cleaning duties.

Ewen kept sweeping the floor, piling up the debris at the far end to be disposed of later. Regardless of the privileged upbringing she imagined he'd had growing up here, he wasn't afraid to do his share of hard work. Bonnie thought back to the day she'd arrived when he'd been out the back doing his lumberjack impression, now here he was sweeping up whilst dressed in his full duke attire. It was no wonder he had women falling at his feet. All he needed was a photo op with a baby on his bare chest and they'd have a stampede at the castle door.

Bonnie made a mental note to suggest a top-less calendar in the new year. There was no way of knowing how he'd take the idea of being a pin-up, but it was bound to get them some new sightseers around the place keen to sneak a peek at the hot duke. She'd just have to get over the idea of other women gawping at him, along with the images of him posing in various states of undress…

Ewen paused and leaned on the top of the broom. 'The family hold a ball every year for all the residents of the village, as well as local dignitaries. It's much more salubrious than to-day's event. A black-tie affair with a champagne reception and formal dinner.'

'Is there waltzing?' She wanted to picture the scene the way she'd always imagined those Regency-style balls, ladies flirting up a storm behind their fans, whilst handsome gentlemen vied to add their names to their dance cards.

Ewen sighed. 'Yes, there's waltzing, and fox-trotting, and my dad was even known to do the highland fling after a wee dram or two of whisky. Can't say I was ever really a part of it. Ruari and I were too young to be allowed to stay up late when I lived here. And, as you know, I didn't spend much time here as an adult.'

'So you're not going to keep up the tradition?' She could see why he wouldn't be inclined to continue with the event, but could understand why people would be upset. It might not earn him any brownie points with the locals if he put an end to something they'd been enjoying for years, at a time when he probably needed all the friends he could get.

'I haven't decided yet. Mrs McKenzie is nagging me about it and she wants me to look for Father's contact list to send out the invitations, but it would be a big commitment. We only just pulled off today, and that was with a wedding planner doing all the organising.'

'Surely Mrs McKenzie will have contact details for people who've worked it before?' She knew it would be a daunting task, but she was sure there would be caterers and musicians, or whoever they used for such an event, who knew the score.

'Oh, yes. I just need to make the call on whether or not it's happening. If I still want to be part of that.' The sag of his shoulders said he didn't, that he wanted to shrug off the ties to his parents, but given his position it was impossible. Living here, taking on his father's title and responsibilities, he would be living in his shadow for ever. Perhaps it would be healthier for him to accept all that came with the role, and do it to the best of his ability, rather than to rail against it. It didn't do anyone any good to hold onto those bad memories or feelings.

'You still have to make a life for yourself here, Ewen. It won't help if you alienate the locals. Perhaps you can still host but put your own twist on things?' She wanted the best for him, and the castle. Not only because her future was tied up in both, but because she *cared*.

'Hmm, we'll see.'

'When is it? You can't put it off for ever.'

He ducked his head, and, looking up at her under his long eyelashes, said, 'Next month.'

Bonnie immediately dropped the now full rubbish bags onto the floor. 'In that case…no more stalling. I'll help you find your father's list of contacts, then we're going to start organising your version of the annual ball.'

'Yes, ma'am.' Ewen let his broom fall to the ground and saluted her.

Bonnie wasn't usually this bossy, but she had a feeling he needed to move on just as much as she had. That could only happen when he confronted his problems. It wasn't easy, but she wasn't going to let him do it alone.

'You can give me the guided tour. I haven't seen much of the place behind the red velvet ropes.' She linked her arm through his, not caring if it took all night to find that book and start making arrangements. Ewen needed it, and she wanted to do something that would make them feel good. Preferably something that didn't involve them getting naked together and messing things up between them.

CHAPTER SEVEN

EWEN KNEW HE was dancing with danger extending his time with Bonnie. Yet when he wasn't with her he felt lonelier than ever. He'd had time on his own in the apartment after Victoria had left, spent weeks in the castle with just the ghosts of the past for company. But that was before Bonnie had arrived. Before he'd got used to having her to talk to, to share dinner with, to think about even when he wasn't with her.

Today had been a success, but it might not have happened if he hadn't had her to push him forward and think about the future of the castle. Even if he wasn't around for long, the place would hopefully still be standing here for another few hundred years. Regardless that he'd effectively be turning his back on his family heritage by selling up, he nevertheless wanted it to survive without him. The only hitch in his plans now was Bonnie.

Not only was he going to upset her when she discovered he intended to sell up and move on, but it was going to be more of a wrench for him now when the time came. He'd thought it would be easy to rid himself of the family home and all the bad memories he associated with it. Being lumbered with it was a headache he'd imagined he'd be happy to shake off. Then Bonnie had moved in and changed everything.

She was part of the fabric of the castle now. He wouldn't want to make a deal on the sale of the place unless he knew she would still be okay. Then there were the new memories he was making with her. The silent, awkward dinners with his parents after Ruari had gone now replaced with thoughts of her in his apartment sharing Italian on his couch. Those lonely nights in his room, staying out of sight to avoid upsetting anyone, fading against the fun he'd had with Bonnie in the kitchen making chocolates.

Then there was that moment on the stairs, leaning in to kiss her. That was what he'd think about every time he climbed the staircase, instead of his mother standing there wailing about the loss of her son and snarling at the one she still had. Bonnie was exorcising his demons one by one. Perhaps he needed to go through the castle room by room with her...

Images of what that could entail flashed in his mind. New fun memories they could have created together if they hadn't stopped themselves from giving into temptation.

Taking her into his father's study and letting her even further into his private life wasn't going to help his resolve. Yet he didn't want to do it alone.

'I haven't touched anything in here yet.' He opened the door for only the second time since he'd come back. This time he stepped inside instead of simply shutting the door on it again.

'Wow. It's like something out of a fairy tale.' Bonnie stood in the middle of the study, spinning around like a kid lost in a fairground.

'I've never really thought about it that way, but I suppose it is impressive.' Ewen tried to look at the place through her perspective. A floor-to-ceiling rainbow of colour-coded books was something he'd taken for granted growing up. Especially when several of the rooms in the castle had their own mini library. A lot of the books had been inherited, some added by his father, none to be touched. And now they were his.

'Feel free to take one whenever you want.'

'Really?' She was already running her fingers down the leather spines, caressing first editions that probably hadn't been read in decades. Touched only by the people who came to carefully clean them every now and then.

'That's what they're supposed to be for. Don't

ask me what we've got, I never had permission to as much as look at them until now.' It seemed absurd now to find he was the owner of the entire collection, free to do with it as he chose. He was surprised his father hadn't made separate provisions for the collection rather than let him take control of it. Perhaps he hadn't hated Ewen as much as he'd thought. Or, more likely, he hadn't expected to die when he had.

'That's a pity. I suppose that was something that had been drummed into your father too. I mean, this collection must go back generations, and, I've got to say, some of your ancestors look pretty fierce to me. I don't imagine they encouraged anyone to touch their things. No offence.' Bonnie gave a nod to the portraits above the marble fireplace of the stern dukes who once ruled the roost. She had a point.

'None taken. They were long before my time. I'd like to think I'm not as...controlling.' He was thinking in terms of the rules of the house, but he could see the impact that word had on Bonnie.

There was a flash of something fearful and disturbing in her eyes, before she moved to his father's desk and focused on it instead. 'I suppose if your father's contact list is going to be anywhere, it would be here, right?'

Ewen moved over beside her. 'Sorry, Bonnie.

I didn't mean to bring up any bad associations for you.'

Her smile as she looked up at him was a little too bright to be believed. 'It's fine. I got out. I got away from him. And I'm here with you.'

'I'm not sure that's any consolation for you.'

'Trust me, being with you is like being at a holiday camp compared to life with Ed.' Those big brown eyes were now glassy with tears, the trauma still there looking back at him.

'What did he do to you, Bonnie?' He kept his voice soft and low, not wanting to spook her, but knowing she needed to get this out.

Although she'd told him something of what had happened, he couldn't help the way she needed him to if he didn't know the trauma she'd gone through. Not that he would push if she wasn't ready to share it with him, but he hoped she was. She was such a different person now from the one she described in her past.

She was silent for what seemed like for ever and he was on the brink of apologising again, deciding to leave her past where it belonged. Then her small voice broke through and smashed his heart.

'They have all sorts of names for it these days. Coercive control, gaslighting, and generally making my life hell. He isolated me from my family. Which was all too easy to do when I'd already

been looking for a way out from my overprotective parents. Talk about out of the frying pan…'
Her bitter laugh was so uncharacteristic it made Ewen angry on her behalf.

'I'm sure he didn't show his true colours when you first met. Men like that are sneaky and manipulative. I've met a few in my time.' The business world was full of egos and megalomaniacs, all out for themselves. He'd seen how they operated, trampling over whoever it took to get what they wanted and make themselves feel good. It didn't make it any easier imagining his strong, feisty Bonnie as a victim of one of those people.

'Yeah. Promised me the world, showered me with gifts, made me think I was moving on to something better. Anyway, I was young and naïve, thought that when he wanted to keep me at home to himself it was his way of showing me he loved me. Even after the first time he hit me, I convinced myself it was for my own good. That I must have failed him and needed to do better if I wanted to keep him.' She talked in such a matter-of-fact manner about the mental and physical abuse it was almost as though she'd disassociated from it, and the person she'd been. Perhaps it was for the best, her way of dealing with it. Ewen, on the other hand, was becoming increasingly distressed at the thought of what she'd been through, and that she'd ever blamed herself.

'None of it was your fault. I hope you realise that. These men thrive on breaking people down. Usually strong ones at that. What happened was a sign of his weakness, not yours.' He wanted to hold her, hug her, show her the tenderness she deserved, but it would be overstepping the mark in all sorts of ways.

'I know. I realised that eventually. After a couple of black eyes, broken ribs, and a split lip. That's why I didn't hang around to start the family he was trying to pressure me into having. I wasn't so far removed from reality that I thought that would be a good idea. I suppose it made me wonder why I was putting up with his behaviour if I wasn't prepared to subject anyone else to it. Anyway, I don't want to let him take up any more room in my life. He's in prison now, where he belongs.'

From that he understood she didn't want to talk about it again. She'd told him her story, and he was grateful that she'd felt able to share it with him. Though he'd winced at the description of her injuries, had got angry at the man who thought he had the right to inflict such horrific damage on such a wonderful person, it wasn't his right to feel any of those things.

He was simply grateful she'd found the strength

to report him and get away for her own sake. It helped him better understand what had brought her here and gave him more of an insight into the amazing person he already knew her to be.

'I understand. We'll never speak of him again, but thank you for sharing that with me. I know how painful it must have been, and I think you're incredibly brave. Onwards and upwards for both of us from now on.' He only hoped when the time came for him to move on from his painful past she would understand too.

'Starting with this annual ball. No more procrastinating, Mr Harris, you need to find this book.' Seemingly done with the topic of her abusive ex, Bonnie got back to the task at hand—busting his chops.

Ewen groaned and set to work searching his father's desk. Something else he'd been forbidden to touch when he was younger. 'He used to do everything at this desk. Opening his mail, meetings with his tenants, writing in his journal.'

'And now it's yours.'

Ewen looked at the fountain pen lying where his father had last left it and the neat pile of papers waiting for his attention. It was like a time capsule, a moment of his father's life captured for ever. Tasks he would never complete.

'I'm not sure I would ever feel comfortable in here. It's a little too formal for me. I'm more a "laptop on my knee in front of the telly" kind of guy.' He couldn't imagine working in here, always thinking his father was looking over his shoulder disapproving of whatever he was doing.

'It seems a shame not to use it. It's such an amazing room.'

'Maybe I'll open it up to the public. After I take out any of his personal papers, of course.' He was sure any visitors would react the same way Bonnie had upon seeing his father's study. They would get a lot more from having access to this room than he would.

That wasn't to say a new owner wouldn't completely gut the place and turn it into a games room if they chose, and there would be nothing he could do about it. A notion that bothered him more now than it used to.

'You haven't gone through any of this yet?' Bonnie began to open the drawers in the desk, revealing stacks of notebooks and Manilla envelopes, all of which he would have to sort through at some stage.

'Not yet. All of the important legal papers were with his solicitor. This is probably his journals and the records to do with his family history. He was big into that. If we empty everything onto the desk, I'll get some boxes tomorrow and pack it all away.' To deal with at a later date.

He flicked through the loose papers sitting on

the desk to make sure there were no outstanding bills, but they'd all been settled. Whether that was his father's doing, or the estate manager, he didn't know.

'He was so organised,' Bonnie remarked as she stacked the neatly labelled files on the desk.

'I don't remember him being like that. The place was usually cluttered with papers everywhere, and I don't think anyone has been in here since he died.' He was sure if Mrs McKenzie had tidied things away she would have mentioned it.

'Perhaps he was getting his affairs in order to make it easier for you to deal with. It's a lot to take on. Especially when you were estranged for so long.' Bonnie's take on his father's sudden predilection for housekeeping hit hard. Although his death had been unexpected, according to Mrs McKenzie, he'd had heart problems in the past, and hadn't been in great health towards the end. Organising his personal affairs so he didn't put Ewen to too much trouble wasn't in keeping with the idea of a father who didn't love him. Perhaps, at the very least, he hadn't hated him as he much as he'd thought.

'Maybe he had an attack of conscience after all these years and realised not everything that happened was my fault.' He couldn't help but feel aggrieved regardless. A better way to show remorse and regret over their lost relationship would have been to reach out before it was too late to make amends. If Ewen had had any hint that he would've been welcomed here he might've been persuaded to visit and at least speak to his father before his death. Instead, he'd remained oblivious to his thoughts and health issues, still an outcast.

'Are you okay?'

He heard the concern in Bonnie's voice before he saw it in her eyes or felt it in the touch of his arm. Until now he'd kept the family circumstances to himself, but she deserved an explanation for the mess she'd walked into, and was now living in. More than that, it was time he finally opened up about what had happened, had to if he ever hoped to move past it, and he knew Bonnie would understand. She knew how it was to walk away from a toxic relationship.

'There's something I haven't told you...' He'd got over the guilt of the accident a long time ago, but he'd lived with other people's condemnation for so long he hesitated before spilling the details.

Then he saw the sympathetic tilt of her head and knew Bonnie would hear him out without judgement.

'The reason I wasn't in contact with my parents for so long was because they blamed me for my brother Ruari's death.' He watched for a flinch, a sign that she was wary of him even before he told her the details, but she simply waited to hear him out.

'I was driving when the crash happened. I'd only just passed my driving test and the roads were icy. The car slid out of control and there was nothing I could do.' Even talking about it now brought him back to that night, the helplessness as he tried to steer the car away from danger, then the horrible crunch of the car hitting the tree, and the jolt as he was thrown forward at the impact. He'd never forget the silence that followed. That terrible quiet that told him his brother was dead.

'It was an accident. Surely your parents understood that.' Bonnie's voice gently brought him back to the present.

Ewen shook his head. 'They were completely blinded by their grief, couldn't bear to even look at me. So I went to university and never looked back. Until now.'

'Perhaps this was your father's way of making amends. By leaving you everything here he was making sure you're set for life.'

'I suppose that's how it looks from the outside, but I'm successful in my own right. I created an app and sold it for enough money that I'd never have to work again if I chose.'

Bonnie's eyes widened at that and Ewen

blushed a little. He didn't make a huge song and dance about his wealth, especially since Victoria had made him more careful about sharing those kinds of personal details. Never knowing who might try to take advantage of him again. In this context, though, it was an important detail.

'Lucky you,' Bonnie said with a grin.

He was aware mentioning his financial status was somewhat tone-deaf given Bonnie's circumstances. 'It's not my intention to boast. I'm just saying my father must have had an ulterior motive in leaving this castle to me. I'm just not sure what that is yet.'

'You're still his son, Ewen. Maybe he realised he was in the wrong and this was his way of showing you that he still cared about you.'

'I love your optimism, but I'm not convinced. My father had years after my mother died to reach out and build some bridges. If he had, things could have been very different.' As it was, Ewen felt only resentment that he'd been forced back to BenCrag.

Bonnie contemplated his take on the matter and seemed to accept it, not putting forward any further argument. Instead, she set to work helping him go through his father's things, looking for the elusive address book.

They systematically went through the papers

on top of the desk before starting on the contents of the drawers.

'Ewen?' Bonnie lifted out an envelope from one of the drawers and handed it to him.

His name was etched in ink on the front in his father's unmistakable scrawl. Ewen's blood ran cold, as though he'd just been touched by icy fingers from beyond the grave. His father was finally reaching out to him for the first time in over a decade after all.

He took the envelope, holding it carefully as though it were a bomb about to go off. For all he knew it might be. His legs unsteady, he collapsed into the leather office chair where his father once sat and stared at the letter, realising that once he opened it there was no going back. Whatever his father had to say to him, it would likely dictate what he thought about him for the rest of his life. There was no way of knowing if it was simply a written account of the blame he felt Ewen deserved for Ruari's death, or regret that they never got to say the final goodbye they should have had in person.

'I don't know if I can…' Good or bad, this was the last thing his father ever had to say to him, and he wasn't sure if he was ready for it. He was glad at least to have Bonnie with him.

She perched on the edge of the desk, a move that would seriously have infuriated his father, but ultimately made him smile. 'Do you want me to do it?'

It was tempting to let her have the dubious honour of opening the letter and reading whatever his father had to say to him. 'No. He left it for me. The least I can do is read it.'

He took a deep breath before attempting to disarm the explosive device beneath his fingertips, sweat breaking out on his forehead. Even Bonnie seemed to be holding her breath, waiting for the fallout from the blast.

If the sight of his father's familiar handwriting hadn't knocked the breath out of him, the *Dear Son* opening did. He dropped the letter on his lap and drew in a shaky breath, trying to compose himself.

'Let me do it.' Bonnie gently reached out and took the letter. He didn't try to stop her, afraid if he read any more he'd break down in front of her. Although she wouldn't want a replica of her violent ex, he doubted she'd be impressed by a tearful, grieving duke either.

'"*Dear Son, If you're reading this, I'm already gone. We didn't get to say goodbye. I didn't quite manage the courage to reach out to you in the end, and for that I'm sorry. Along with everything else.*"'

Bonnie looked up to see how he was handling it so far. She knew he was doing the macho male thing, thinking it was a sign of weakness to show any emotion. Not that he was especially good at hiding it, nor would she expect him to be. This was a big deal.

She hadn't been aware of his difficult family circumstances, but it must've been horrible bearing the unjust burden of his brother's death. It wasn't fair that he'd shouldered the blame all these years, lost his parents along with his brother. It was an accident. Although she'd lost all of her family and friends too after one stupid mistake in the form of her ex, so she guessed that gave them one more thing in common.

It was also where the similarities ended. He wouldn't get proper closure, or a chance to repair those damaged relationships, but she could. Maybe one day, when she was stronger, successful, and her ex was nothing more to her than a bad memory, she would go back waving an olive branch. It wasn't too late.

Being estranged from her parents too, she knew how difficult it was not to have them for important milestones, or emotional support when needed. She knew if she had any sort of contact from her own parents asking her to come home, she'd be reduced to a sobbing mess.

Ewen gripped the sides of his chair and waited for her to continue, apparently steeling himself for more.

"'I know the accident wasn't your fault, and deep down your mother knew that too. We just couldn't seem to find a way out of our grief, and I'm ashamed to say we took it out on you. These last years on my own have made me reflect on how we treated you, and how we let you down. I wanted to apologise to you, Ewen, and often thought about contacting you. In the end, I was too much of a coward. You were doing so well on your own. I could see you didn't need me to bring you down. Yes, I've kept track of your achievements over the years, and if it's not too late I want to say I'm proud of you. I'm proud that you're my son.'"

Bonnie heard her voice cracking and took a moment to clear her throat. It was evident this had been written by a man full of regret in his last days, but still unable to show his son how much he loved him. It was a tragedy all around.

The least Ewen deserved was to hear what his father had to say without her crying all over him.

"'I hope you can forgive me, and your mother, for everything. I suppose it's a fitting punishment for me to die believing you still hate me, but for your own sake, Ewen, don't live the rest of your life with hate in your heart. Your mother was bitter after Ruari's death, it tainted everything, and that's what killed her in the end. So, I'm leaving you everything, hoping you'll realise

I did love you, and that I trust you to make all the right decisions when it comes to the castle. I'm only sorry I left it too late to make amends in person. I wish you a long and prosperous life, son. But, more importantly, I hope it's a happy one. With love from your father."'

As Bonnie finished reading the letter aloud, the room fell into silence, both of them processing the contents. Ewen dropped his head, the weight of trying to stay strong apparently becoming too much.

It was instinctive to move closer to him, wrap her arms around his neck, and offer some comfort. The same way he'd done for her in the past. He buried his head against her stomach and hugged her closer. He didn't make a sound, but she knew he was hurting. As much as he'd needed to hear that apology, it wasn't going to bring back his father or repair their relationship. It would only add to his regrets.

'He loved you, Ewen. Just hold onto that.'

He tilted up his face to look at her, those blue eyes so full of pain and grief that he could no longer hide. 'And now he's gone, who do I have?'

Bonnie recognised that loneliness and her heart ached for him. It didn't seem fair to let him think there was no one left in the world to care for him when she knew otherwise.

'Me,' she said, cupping his face in her hands,

and dropping a soft kiss on his lips. They'd been dancing around the attraction, and their growing feelings—at least she had, and Ewen's actions to date would suggest he was having the same problem. Circumstances had thrown them together and they'd found comfort in one another. She wondered why that was such a bad thing, given the ordeals they'd both been through recently.

Ewen pulled her closer, until she slid off the edge of the desk and was sitting astride his lap. There were no words needed, only actions. They both wanted, *needed*, this, and it didn't look as though either of them wanted to stop it this time. She wrapped her arms around his neck, he grabbed her backside with both hands, and they let their mouths find each other again.

Bonnie leaned into the kiss, into Ewen, letting him carry her away on that wave of passion she'd known was waiting to crash over both of them. Their want for one another apparent in their grinding bodies, and insistent mouths. She didn't want to listen to that nagging inner voice trying to protect her from herself, insisting that this was a bad idea. So she focused instead on the sensations Ewen was introducing her body to. The languid kisses that she couldn't get enough of, and that ache at her very core she knew only he could remedy.

She was so lost in the taste of him, the hot feel of his mouth meshed with hers, that it took her a moment to register that he'd stood up and was setting her back down on the desk. When she attempted to extricate herself from him, worried that she'd missed his cue that the moment was over, he grabbed her legs and wrapped them back around his waist.

'I didn't want us to stop. I just thought we needed a bit more room.' He was kissing her neck, slipping the straps of her dress down her bare shoulders, and doing everything to steal her breath away.

Then he cupped her breasts in his hands, and almost rendered her catatonic. His assured touch, combined with his hot breath on her skin, was just the thing to make her remember she was more than a victim, or a survivor. She was still very much a woman with needs.

With greedy hands of her own, she stripped away his shirt to explore the dip and rise of his muscular physique. Marvelling at the hard muscle and solid strength beneath her fingertips. The very essence of masculinity. Even more so because he didn't feel the need to assert his dominance over her like every other man in her life. Sufficient to turn her on even if he hadn't unclipped her bra and was now…oh…

She tilted her head back as waves of ecstasy

crashed over her, Ewen sucking one nipple, then the other. Arousal was coursing so hard and fast through her body she thought it would burst through her skin. Then everything stopped. Ewen took a step back, abandoning her, leaving her restless and frustrated.

'What's wrong?' Her voice was husky with unfulfilled need and concern as she fought to remember Ewen's feelings in all of this. He was bound to be emotional and confused, and perhaps she'd taken advantage of his moment of vulnerability.

He fixed her with his cutest hot-guy smile. 'Given the circumstances, doing this on my father's desk seems a little disrespectful. And weird. Do you mind if we take this somewhere else?'

Bonnie's relief was quickly overtaken by her returning desire as he wrapped her legs back around his waist, her arms around his neck, and lifted her from the desk.

'Not at all,' she gasped, her breasts pushing against his bare chest and stoking that fire within her. That intimate contact, a promise of more, only pushed her further towards the brink of madness with every step he took.

Ewen carried her into his bedroom and laid her on his bed, coming down onto the mattress with her. Here in his own space he seemed to lose what was left of his inhibitions, kissing her all over as he stripped her naked. Leaving her exposed and wanting.

She watched with increasing hunger whilst he discarded the rest of his clothes, reaching for him once he was magnificently naked before her. He left her momentarily to find some protection, giving her the opportunity to marvel at his naked form. All honed muscle, no doubt from the manual labour he wasn't afraid to do. A true Scottish warrior who deserved his fine physique to be captured for prosperity on the side of a shortbread tin. Albeit a more PG image.

He had that tall, proud body she could imagine striding through the highlands, and for tonight, at least, it was all hers.

Ewen caught her watching and smirked, prowling along the bed back towards her.

'You look pleased with yourself,' Bonnie remarked, anticipation of what was to come making her a little nervous. Her sheltered life before her ex meant she had scant experience in the bedroom department, save for what she'd had with Ed. Given the playful, passionate lead-up with Ewen so far, she was beginning to realise she had a lot to learn. And that she'd been missing out.

'Just enjoying being objectified. You're looking at me the way the wedding guests were eyeing your chocolate today.'

'It's true. I haven't had a thing to eat for ages,' she said, shifting her body so it was perfectly positioned beneath his.

Ewen looked stricken by her comment. 'I'm sorry. I didn't think. We can go get something now if you need to eat.'

Bonnie loved that he was so considerate, if a little slow on the uptake. Willing to set aside his wants to make sure she was okay. A real man. Though clearly her pillow talk needed some work.

When he straightened up as though to leave her, she moved quickly, wrapping her arms around his neck to keep him anchored to the bed with her.

'The only thing I'm hungry for is you.' She kissed him with renewed fervour to prove he was the only thing on her mind.

He sagged against her, the weight of him reassuring her he wasn't going anywhere unless she requested it. And she hoped neither of them were leaving his bed for the foreseeable future. Not when he was worshipping her with his tongue, and his mouth, touching her with a tenderness she'd never experienced before.

Every soft kiss as he travelled down her body, covering all erogenous zones, taught her a new way of loving. Her ex hadn't cared too much about her needs, or feelings, helping himself as though she was nothing but a possession to be used at his will. Now she looked back, sex had never been a particularly enjoyable part of their relationship. Simply something expected of her to keep him happy. To show him she loved him. She didn't recall ever receiving the same consideration in return.

Ewen, on the other hand, appeared to be on a mission to drive her wild. In a good way. With all of those feel-good endorphins colliding with this all-new lust coursing through her veins, she no longer had any control over what was happening to her. Though in these circumstances she was happy to let Ewen take the driving seat. He seemed to know what she wanted, needed, and was determined to serve it to her on the tip of his tongue.

Bonnie arched up off the bed with a gasp as he dipped inside her core, holding her steady with his hands on her thighs. Her climax took her by surprise with the speed and force with which it came, leaving her head spinning, and her body limp.

'You okay?' Ewen asked, before dotting kisses along her inner thighs, starting that fluttering sensation across her skin all over again.

'Yeah... I'm just...' She didn't know how

to thank him for making her feel loved without sounding pathetic. 'I'm, er, not used to this, that's all.'

It wasn't easy to admit she was practically a virgin, that there were still a lot of unknowns, uncharted territory, for her when it came to sex. Bonnie felt a flush spread from the top of her head down to her toes, the heat of her embarrassment tinging her pale skin pink.

Ewen frowned, not quite understanding. Then she watched as realisation dawned and he let loose several choice words about her ex. He came up to lie beside her.

'I don't want to do anything you don't want to do. I just want to make you feel good.' With a gentle kiss on the lips, and the slow sweep of her hips with his hand, he started that build-up of pressure inside her all over again.

'Oh, I don't want you to stop...' Emboldened by Ewen's desire to keep her happy, she reached between their bodies and took hold of him. His gasp at her confident power play only encouraged more of this new, wanton Bonnie.

She moved her hand along his shaft, revelling in the evidence of his desire for her, and the ragged breaths she was drawing from Ewen as he fought to regain control. It was powerful knowing she could make him feel this way about her. They might regret this in the morning, when they were thinking clearly enough to realise the consequences. That it was going to make working and living together complicated. For tonight, at least, she wanted to forget he was her boss, and for a little while at least pretend she was the one in charge.

Ewen was doing his best to treat Bonnie as tenderly as she deserved. Though she was making that a challenge when she was touching him the way she was, straddling his lap now, and testing his restraint to the max.

After hearing a little about her selfish ex, he wanted this to be good for her. He knew he was probably the rebound guy in this scenario, but he couldn't ask for more than that. To do so would put their working relationship in jeopardy and he was coming to rely on Bonnie more and more. Tonight had proved that. He'd opened up to her more about his family than he ever had with anyone else, but that was also why this couldn't be any more than sex. Relationships never worked out for him and he wasn't ready to lose Bonnie when he'd just found her.

His father's letter had knocked him for six. He'd never expected an apology, especially posthumously. It was bittersweet to receive one when it was too late to do anything about it. They'd wasted so much time and thrown away a relationship. Giving up on one another too easily, at a time when they'd probably needed each other more than ever. With his father's health in decline, and Ewen's relationship with Victoria on the critical list too, they could have leaned on each other.

Now there was no going back. He didn't want to make the same mistake again with someone he cared about. Yes, despite years of telling himself otherwise, he'd still loved his parents. Since they'd seemed happier without him in their lives, it had been easier to convince himself he didn't need them. It was only now his father had confessed it was fear that had kept him from reaching out that Ewen could admit the same. Except he also hadn't wanted to face the same rejection, which had bordered on hatred, that he'd received at the time of Ruari's death. So he'd stayed away, and now it was too late to repair the damage.

It was a bitter pill to swallow. And a reminder not to waste time. He didn't want to live with any more regrets. Tonight he wanted to be with Bonnie, to express those growing feelings he had towards her. All the self-recriminations could wait. He just wanted to feel good, and it seemed as though Bonnie was overdue some loving too. Although she was doing her best to make him forget any chivalrous behaviour, grinding against him. Teasing him until he was ready to explode.

Then she bore down on him, joining their bodies together, and Ewen knew he was lost to her. With one hand braced on his chest, the other stroking between his thighs, Bonnie had him at her mercy. It was all he could do not to flip her onto her back and thrust into her like the Neanderthal she brought out in him. But she needed this. She needed to be in control. To find out what she liked. To learn how to enjoy sex, and no longer feel as though it was something merely to be endured.

It was part of life he certainly enjoyed. Especially right now with this firecracker riding him and discovering the joys for herself. Head thrown back in ecstasy, her breath no more than excited pants. Even if he wasn't aroused beyond rational thought, the sight of her taking pleasure from his body was certainly an aphrodisiac. He needed that boost after the way Victoria had so cruelly discarded him. This brought a whole new dimension to his relationship with Bonnie. Bonnie, who was sweet and attractive, and so damn sexy.

Her breathy moans as she grew closer and closer to the end finally undid him. Ewen thrust his hips up to meet hers and forced a gasp from her. So he did it again, and again, until his blood was thundering in his veins and Bonnie was crying out her release. As she crashed over the edge and slowly came back to earth, rocking gently now, he was finally able to take control once more.

He shifted their bodies, until Bonnie was beneath him, and drove home again. She tightened her inner muscles around him and shattered what was left of his composure. That overwhelming bliss managed to blot out all the pain he'd endured tonight, leaving him satisfied and content to lie with Bonnie, the miracle worker. He couldn't help but think she might become a habit he wasn't going to be able to break. However, like all vices, he worried that his desire for another fix might begin to affect all other aspects of his life.

For now, though, he was going to enjoy the high.

'What are we doing, Bonnie?' he asked, brushing her tangled hair from her face.

The satisfied smile across her kiss-swollen lips was tempting his weary body back to life already.

'If you don't know that then you're more naïve than I am.'

That made him laugh. 'You know what I mean. Tonight has been amazing, but what happens tomorrow?'

Ewen didn't want things to get awkward between them, the dynamic changed for ever, and not in a good way.

'Well, I'm not the boss, but I think it's pretty much the same as every day. We open the doors, people pay their entrance fee, you charm them, and I try to get them to buy some chocolate.'

'Ha-ha. Very funny. I just… I don't want to ruin things.' He had a lot to deal with in the not-too-distant future: the clean-up, the ball, and the emotional fallout from his father's letter still to come. Things he could do on his own, but would much prefer to have Bonnie by his side for if he could. She made everything better.

She turned onto her side and fixed him with a serious stare. 'I don't see why this has to be anything. We don't need to label spending time together. I doubt either of us is ready to jump into any kind of relationship. Surely we're adult enough not to make a big deal of just sleeping together. I don't want anything serious.'

'Does that mean we can still have some fun?' He threw an arm around her waist and pulled her closer, hooking her thigh over his so their most intimate parts were flush once more.

Ewen knew he could never get enough of her. This was exactly where he wanted to be, with her full breasts pressed tightly against his chest, her body wrapped around his. Where he felt wanted.

He didn't want this to be the last time.

'Keep it casual?'

'If that means you'll stay the night without either of us panicking that the other will read more into it, then yes, let's keep things casual. By day we'll be mild-mannered work colleagues, at night, red-hot secret lovers.'

'Ooh, I like the sound of that.' Bonnie started kissing her way along his neck, then drew his earlobe into her mouth.

Ewen felt a familiar stirring in his groin and he was glad they were in no rush to get back to reality. Tomorrow, they could deal with any repercussions he was currently not letting have access to his brain. Because that was totally consumed with thoughts of how they were going to spend these next few hours together.

CHAPTER EIGHT

'ARE YOU SURE you don't want to get in with me?'
Bonnie was lying with her head against the old
copper bucket-style tub, which Ewen had filled
with soothing hot water for her tired body.

'I'm not sure there's any room left for me.' He
scooped some water from the bath in the gold-
rimmed ewer he'd taken from the dressing table,
and poured it over her hair.

With the only light in the bathroom coming
from the candles he'd lit around the tiled room,
the scent of rose and honey in the air, he was ro-
mancing her after the fact. The opposite of how
her ex had worked. A sign that he wasn't pretending to be someone he wasn't just to get his
own way, because she was his any time he chose.
He'd proven himself to be supportive, considerate, and loving. All the things Ed had pretended
to be in order for her to fall in love with him.
Bonnie just had to make sure she kept some perspective with Ewen. She didn't want to fall for
someone who didn't want her in his life. That

would almost be as tragic as staying with someone who'd emotionally and physically damaged her. Just a different form of abuse. Albeit self-inflicted.

'I'll make room.' Though she was enjoying her impromptu pampering session. After another enthusiastic bout of bedroom gymnastics, Ewen had insisted on drawing her a bath.

She wasn't some damsel who needed taking care of, but it was nice to have someone treat her so well. He was good for her body and soul. A soothing balm for the trauma scars her ex had left on her. Ewen was helping her undo some of the damage, showing her she was worth desiring, caring about. That being with someone didn't have to mean pain and upset. He gave her space to work through her feelings, and at the same time was there for her when she needed company or support.

Keeping things casual reduced expectations on both sides and she was happy enough with that for now. It was early days, for her relationship not only with Ewen, but with herself. She needed time to trust again, to explore the sort of romantic entanglement she did, or didn't, want. Ewen was showing her a kindness and tenderness she wasn't used to and she was happy to simply enjoy his attentions in the meantime. Ed might not be representative of all men, but that didn't mean she was ready to jump into something serious with anyone else again. Some time exploring her freedom was enough for now.

'It's okay. I think it's about time someone took care of you for a change. Besides, we both need a recovery period. You can have too much of a good thing, you know.'

'Really? Because I think I have a lot of lost time to make up...' Whilst she didn't want to be a slave to another man's whims, her aching body was still craving Ewen. She hadn't known someone could ever make her feel this way, and it made her sad for the version of her who'd put up with so much less for so long. Now she knew she was worth more than being a punchbag for a bully, she would never accept anything less than the way Ewen treated her. Like a duchess.

These past months, she'd proved to herself that she was independent, and courageous, and all the other words the women's charity had used to try and instil some confidence into her. It was only coming to the castle and setting up her new life that had helped her to start believing it. She didn't need anyone else to give her life meaning. Although Ewen had shown her that sometimes it could still be fun to share her life when it suited her. Like tonight.

She felt like a born-again virgin, discovering sex for the first time. Keen to explore every new position, along with her new-found sexuality. It had been an awakening, one she was glad to have had, but that also worried her. What if Ewen had spoiled her for ever? If he was the new standard, any other man had a lot to live up to. She wasn't even sure she'd want anyone else. The memories they were making now might be enough to sustain her for ever. That was why she didn't want it to end.

'We're not in any hurry, are we? Casual means just that. We can pick this up again whenever we choose.' Ewen took a detour with the soapy sponge he'd been washing her down with, paying particular attention to her nipples, before dipping lower under the water.

She closed her eyes and gave herself over to the sensation. 'Hmm, we might have to hold that thought. I think I'm going to have to take that time out we talked about.'

Although her mind was willing, her body pleasantly numb, she'd clearly reached her orgasm limit for the night. A yawn slipped out of her mouth unbidden, reminding her that it had been a busy, energetic day.

'Right. I think we're done for the night.' Ewen grabbed a couple of towels and helped her out of the bath. Once she was sufficiently dried, he wrapped her in a big fluffy white robe.

'You have your own private spa in here,' she

teased, then found herself wondering how many other women had enjoyed the same treatment. Though it was none of her business, and she had no claim on Ewen, she wanted to believe he'd done this only for her. That she was special.

'I guess there are some perks to living in a castle. I just haven't availed myself of them in a long time. We do a personal chauffeur service too,' he said, putting her mind at ease that this hadn't simply been part of his usual seduction technique.

'Well, I'm not planning on going anywhere for the foreseeable future.' She gave another yawn and stretched as he tied the robe around her waist.

'Oh, I think you are.' With a mischievous glint in his eye, he scooped her up in his arms.

Her little scream of protest in response was in contrast to the way she was wrapping her arms around his neck and snuggling into his chest. She'd never been so romanced, felt so wanted and sexy, and she had Ewen to thank for everything.

The only blot in her perfect romantic fantasy was when Ewen kept walking past his bed and down the hallway, carrying her away from the prospect of more time with him tonight.

'Where are you taking me?'

'To bed. Your bed.'

'Oh.' A cloak of disappointment settled around her shoulders that it had all come to an end. He'd made the decision for both of them. Despite their talk about continuing on a casual basis, who knew when they'd get to do this again, or if they could ever hope to replicate the magic they'd shared tonight?

'You need some rest. So do I, come to think of it.' He gave a self-deprecating laugh. 'Besides, we don't want Mrs McKenzie seeing us slipping in and out of one another's rooms, do we?'

'I guess not.' He had a point. She was already the outsider on the staff, and, though they were pleasant enough, she didn't want to alienate herself by becoming too cosy with the boss. He too was still trying to make his mark here, had a lot to prove, and it probably wouldn't do his credibility any good if it was public knowledge he was sleeping with the hired help.

It didn't mean she wasn't going to feel the loss once he left her here alone.

Ewen set her gently down on the bed and went to take his leave.

'Can you stay with me for a little while? At least until I fall asleep?' She didn't want to appear needy, but this was the first night since leaving her ex, maybe even before then, when she hadn't felt alone. It would be nice, just for once, to fall asleep knowing someone was there with her. Someone she didn't have to fear.

'Sure.' He climbed onto the bed so they were lying face to face.

'Thank you. It's been a while since I felt this safe and happy. I just want to make it last.' The fact that Ewen hadn't already run in the opposite direction from all of her baggage made her comfortable with the admission. He knew about her past and he was more understanding about her needs than she could ever have hoped for.

'I get it. It's no fun going to bed alone at night.' He plumped up the pillow and settled in beside her, not in any hurry to leave her at all.

'Why aren't you married?' She hadn't intended to say it out loud, but it was hard to understand why someone like Ewen hadn't been snapped up. He was handsome, rich, had a title, and a conscience, all of which were rare enough, but he was also kind and loving. If she hadn't just come out of her nightmare of a relationship, she would probably be hoping for something long-term herself. But she didn't know if she'd ever want that with anyone. If she could ever trust a man enough to completely open up and share her life with him. She had a feeling this was the closest she'd ever get.

Ewen sighed, and he seemed to drift off somewhere else for a moment. A place that tightened his jaw and robbed him of his dreamy smile. Bonnie was already regretting the question.

'Not my choice. I did think it was on the cards, along with a family of my own. I thought those things were important to Victoria too, but I was wrong. It turned out she was more interested in my bank account, or, more specifically, one that was bigger than mine. She didn't want to move here with me, and found herself another man to fund the life she was accustomed to in London.'

'I'm so sorry. Clearly she wasn't the right woman for you if she didn't appreciate the man you are.' More fool this Victoria if she didn't realise what she'd thrown away. It was hard to find a good one like Ewen, and he certainly deserved being treated better than a cash machine.

'Story of my life.' He had that bone-weary tone she was familiar with. That feeling that nothing was ever going to improve. Luckily she knew that wasn't true.

'So you've no ties left in London?'

'Nope. I sold everything to come here. There's nothing left for me in the city any more.' Although she was sorry he'd endured the pain of a bitter break-up, she couldn't help but be happy that his life was here now. His future was wrapped up in the castle along with hers for the time being.

'What about you? I know you left a bad relationship behind, but you still have family don't you?'

Bonnie screwed her face up. It was a difficult subject, not least after Ewen's discovery about his own father tonight. 'It's complicated. It was my father who taught me everything about being a chocolatier. I spent weekends and holidays working in the shop, helping him with his latest creations. He made everything himself and our whole house smelled of melted chocolate. It was heavenly. Looking back, my parents treated me like their little princess, but instead of appreciating their love, I decided it was suffocating. I wanted to prove I was grown up, no longer their little girl. Then Ed came along… I wouldn't hear a word against him, packed my bags and left. I haven't spoken to my parents since I moved out.'

'Is there any hope for a reconciliation?'

'Honestly, I don't know. I never thought I'd want anything to do with them again. They tried to warn me about getting involved with Ed, but as far as I was concerned, I was right and they were wrong. Of course, I know differently now, and I suppose, if my father reached out the way yours did, there might be a glimmer of hope for us as a family. Some day I might even find the courage to swallow my pride and make that first move…'

'Don't let that prevent you from getting your family back. My situation should be a cautionary tale. I left it too late, don't make the same mistake.'

'We're a right pair, aren't we?' Bonnie moved in for one last cuddle, thankful she had someone, at least for a while, who understood her circumstances, who'd gone through something similar. It made her realise she wasn't some sort of freak who couldn't manage any sort of normal relationship. All families had their issues, but maybe she had a chance of resolving hers. She wondered if by setting up her own chocolate shop she'd been trying to recreate the innocence and security of her childhood, before Ed had destroyed everything.

'At least we have each other for now.' He hugged her close and kissed the top of her head.

The only thing spoiling the moment, that feeling of security and bliss, was *for now*. Right now, she didn't want this to ever end.

Ewen nuzzled into Bonnie's mussed hair, the scent from last night's bath evoking some very happy memories. Spooning her naked body with his was the perfect way to start the day. He didn't know when her robe had been dispensed of, but he was grateful for the curve of her buttocks now resting against his groin. She began to stir as he kissed her neck, shifting her position ever so slightly, but enough to tease his body wide awake.

'I hope you're well rested,' he whispered into her ear, gaining a little shiver in response.

'Hmm mmm.'

He'd barely had time to congratulate himself for taking the next step with Bonnie, when he heard voices downstairs. Followed by the sound of a vacuum cleaner. He sat bolt upright.

'What time is it?'

Bonnie groped for her phone and showed him the screen as she fought to open her eyes.

'Seven o'clock?' He swore and tossed back the covers.

'You stayed all night?'

'I didn't mean to.' He swore again. 'Mrs McKenzie has her own key. She probably let the cleaning crew in.'

'A cleaning crew?' she asked, an eyebrow raised at the admission.

He'd known all along they were coming to clear up after last night's revelry, but when Bonnie had offered her services, he'd seen a chance for them to be alone again and taken it. 'Er, yes. So sue me for wanting to spend more time with you. Anyway, I'm not sure it would be a good look if I was caught naked in bed with a member of staff.'

It was his own fault. He should have left her in her bed and gone to his own room. That was more in keeping with the idea of a casual fling than crawling into bed beside her and cuddling until they'd both fallen asleep. It had just felt so good, the best night's sleep he'd had since moving home. Warning signs that he was getting too comfortable with this arrangement already. If he was going to have the best of both worlds, being with Bonnie, without risking his heart, he had to keep to the boundaries of their casual arrangement.

'Take the robe, or you'll cause even more of a scandal.' Bonnie failed to suppress her amusement as he paced the room naked, wondering how he was going to get out of this.

Ewen grabbed up the robe from the floor and threw it on to cover his modesty.

'I'm sorry. I have to run. I'll see you later, okay?' He paused for one last kiss, aware he wouldn't get to touch her again for the rest of the day. It was going to be torture when he knew every inch of her amazing body now, how soft her lips were, and how well they fitted against his. All of which wasn't going to help him avoid embarrassing himself in front of his staff right now.

'Yes, boss.' Bonnie saluted him with a smile that made him want to slide back into bed beside her and forget about everything outside the bedroom door.

With every ounce of strength in him he opened the door and walked out.

The sound of real life going on downstairs filtered upward. The castle coming to life reminded him that he had priorities over his libido. He crept down the corridor, body pressed to the wall, trying to keep the robe closed so he didn't accidentally expose himself. The scene was probably like something out of a farce, but it made a change from tragedy.

His night with Bonnie had been incredible, something they had been building up to for a while. That attraction sizzling away until it was sure to catch fire, and it had. Spectacularly. However, there was a part of him that wondered if it had also been a way to block out the earlier revelation of his father's letter. A nice distraction for a time, but without Bonnie in his arms his mind was already beginning to think about less appealing things than the sexy curve of her hips under his fingertips.

She wasn't going to be there all day, every day, to take his mind off the time he'd wasted, the mistakes made, and the regrets he was going to have to live with. He was going to have to find another way to deal with this renewed grief.

* * *

Ewen showered and changed as quickly as he could to take up his rightful position, overseeing the work going on in the castle, instead of hiding away pretending it wasn't happening.

'Morning, Mrs McKenzie. You're in early this morning. No hangover?' he teased the housekeeper who looked as though she'd slept standing upright last night, wearing the same crisp grey tweed, and not a hair out of place. Whereas he was sure he had bags under his eyes and had thrown on the first pair of jeans and tee shirt he'd found.

She turned her head away from the cleaning crew she was supervising in the function room to give him a withering look. The same one she used to give him when he was younger after he and Ruari had been caught doing something they shouldn't. Like the time she'd found them putting salt in the sugar bowl before one of their parents' big fancy dinner parties. Mrs McKenzie never had to raise her voice to get him to confess to anything, or make him feel bad about his actions. She only had to give him the look.

She turned away again. Point made that she didn't think he was humorous. 'We have to be ready for opening. The whole place doesn't shut down after one event.'

'I'll remember that. It's hard to get used to

treating this place as a business rather than a home. Though I don't know if it was ever that either...'

Mrs McKenzie tutted. 'You boys never knew how lucky you were. I know your parents took out their grief on you after your brother died, but they loved you. Your father would never have left you all of this if he didn't.'

'I know. I found a letter he left me in his study last night. Too late for me to do anything about it, but he finally apologised.'

Mrs McKenzie dropped her folded arms and stiff upper lip as she faced him. The tears in her grey eyes making her look more human than her usual ice-queen appearance.

'You two were as stubborn as one another. I lost count of the amount of times I tried to get him to contact you. He read me every article about your business success. He was so proud of you.'

'If only he'd told me that. I might have come home sooner.'

'I think he was afraid of you rejecting him. He might have looked gruff on the outside, but he was sensitive. That's why the loss of your brother hit so hard. Don't hate him.'

'I don't. Not any more. That's why I've decided to go ahead with the annual ball in his honour.' It was his way of trying to make peace with the past, as well as giving him something to occupy his thoughts other than Bonnie.

Mrs McKenzie clapped her hands together in an uncharacteristic display of enthusiasm. 'That's great! Oh, there's so much to organise… what about your father's address book? Did you find it yet? We're going to have to get invitations sent out, and book caterers…'

'No… I er, I got distracted by the letter.' He tried not to think about what had followed, not when he was determined to keep his personal life separate from his position at the castle. At least during the day.

'Well, why don't we go find it now? There's no time to waste.' A smiling Mrs McKenzie hooked her arm through his and started walking towards his father's study.

There seemed little point in resisting now he'd committed to the idea of having the ball. He'd been putting it off, unwilling to deal with the emotional baggage lying in that room, but since confronting it with Bonnie, there was no reason to avoid the place any more.

It was only when they entered the room he started to panic. Mostly about any evidence of their passionate tryst they might have left behind last night.

'We…er… I already went through his desk.' He moved quickly to gather the pages and files that had hit the floor in the midst of their late night clinch.

'So I see.' She arched a thin eyebrow, surveying the scene, with Ewen hoping she didn't realise what had actually gone on. That she didn't see the butt-shaped space between the papers scattered on the desk, or at least mistook it for destruction by a grieving son.

'I think there's a filing cabinet over there somewhere. You could try that, and I'll tidy this.' He set to work tidying the mess he and Bonnie had made last night, memories coming thick and fast, and making him ache for her all over again.

Mrs McKenzie moved slowly, eyeing him suspiciously. Just the way she used to do when he and Ruari had been up to no good. She always knew when he was hiding something. In a lot of ways she'd been more of a mother figure to him growing up than his own parent. After the crash, she'd been the one to hug him, to hold him when he'd cried, and reassure him it wasn't his fault. It was his own mother and father who'd convinced him otherwise.

'I'm sorry I didn't keep in touch with you either, Mrs McKenzie. You were always good to me, and you've made my transition here easier than it probably would have been without you.'

He watched her face soften with a smile.

'Things were complicated. I knew you weren't

at fault for what had happened, but your parents were too grief-stricken at the time to see things clearly. My loyalties had to remain with your parents. I'm sorry you were left on your own to deal with everything.'

The pain he saw in her eyes was disconcerting for a woman who'd never been anything but a pillar of strength. It only made his heart ache a little more, realising that he hadn't been the only one hurting this whole time.

Without a family of her own, their housekeeper had devoted her life to the castle and its dysfunctional residents for as long as Ewen could remember. The only one here for his father's dying days, holding things together until his reluctant replacement took over. Even now, she was the one Ewen was turning to for guidance in his new role.

'That's my job. To keep this place standing.'

Strictly speaking, that was the estate manager's job, but everyone knew Mrs McKenzie was really the one in charge. The estate manager had apparently been drafted in when his father had opened the castle up to visitors and the workload had become too much. Not that she would ever have admitted any such thing. Still, he appreciated her sticking around even in the most difficult of circumstances, when she was likely grieving too.

'Thank you for being there for him at the end.' He was glad she'd stayed for his father's sake as much as his own, knowing she would have been a comfort, as well as a practical influence.

It had crossed his mind that she might have had something to do with the farewell letter, a final cleansing of his father's conscience, which he was sure had helped his father die at peace. The way she'd pushed him about looking for the address book might have been a cover to get him to come in here and find it. He supposed it wouldn't have had the same impact if she'd just handed it to him. He'd needed to be ready, in the right headspace to deal with it. It had taken being with Bonnie to get him where he'd needed to be. He just didn't want to come to rely on her. Not when he was going to be moving on again.

He hadn't changed his mind about that, despite his night with Bonnie. If anything, it had only cemented that idea that he had to leave. Becoming too attached to her, to the castle, was pain waiting to happen. At the minute she was exploring her independence, finding her way in the world again, and losing his heart to her was a bad idea when she might decide she didn't want it. He didn't have a good track record when it came to personal attachments. It was safer for him, and his heart, to keep to the original plan and sell up when the time came.

'I know he wasn't always the father you deserved, Ewen, but he was a good man. He filled this place with so many guests and visitors in an attempt to fill that hole in his heart left by you. Don't get me wrong, I know that's not your fault, but he did miss you. And your brother. I'm happy you're going ahead with the ball in his honour. He would've loved that.' She patted him on the arm.

'I'm just sorry we didn't get a chance to make up when he was here. I want to do him proud.'

'As long as you do your best for this place, and for the family name, I'm sure he will be.'

Her words were like knives jabbing at his conscience. She clearly wasn't aware of the stipulation his father had made in his will. That the only reason Ewen was even at the castle was because he'd been forced into it, and he planned to sell it on once the year was up. It probably wasn't the best thing for the castle, or the family legacy, but he was sure it was the right thing for him. Or at least he had been until recently. The longer he spent here, the more complicated things became.

'We'll start with the ball and see how things go from there. All I can do is try.' He didn't want to commit to anything beyond that when it might serve as a farewell party too.

'I'm sure that's all your father is asking of you

too. Just don't let any distractions get in the way of that.' She nodded towards the mess still littered on the desk with that knowing look, and Ewen felt the heat rise in his cheeks.

Warning received loud and clear. This might be only a casual fling with Bonnie, but it was already interfering with the running of the castle. His focus had to be on making it a viable business proposition for the next owner, leaving it in the best possible position so he wouldn't spend the rest of his life feeling guilty about everything he'd walked away from. Perhaps he needed to pull the brakes on his love life now before everything spun out of control. He owed his father that at least.

Ewen knew he couldn't afford to get carried away by this thing with Bonnie for his own sake too. Their connection had happened so quickly, perhaps he needed to slow things down and take stock of what he was really getting himself into. He was drawn to Bonnie for the type of person she was, but he couldn't be sure if it was the same for her. Perhaps her circumstances had coloured her judgement. He'd been the one to offer her a way out after her ex had left her in such a precarious position after all. Either way, he had to be careful that he didn't get too attached to Bonnie, only to end up wounded and alone again.

From now on it was strictly sex. No cuddling until the morning, or thinking about her when he should be planning his future away from Ben-Crag.

His aim was to leave it behind for ever, not find reason to stay.

'I should go.'

Bonnie had barely got her breath back from another mind-blowing orgasm before Ewen was scrambling out of bed and grabbing his clothes. She'd known what she was getting into by agreeing to a casual fling, but it was beginning to feel like more of a series of one-night stands when he left so soon after sex. It had been a couple of weeks since they got together and at first it had been exciting, snatching kisses out of sight of everyone, sneaking in and out of each other's rooms at night. But, despite her promise not to let her feelings get in the way, she wanted more.

'You don't have to. We're adults. Staying overnight doesn't have to mean anything. No one needs to know.' Bonnie didn't want to seem desperate, practically begging him to be with her, but she felt as though he was pulling away from her.

As much as she was enjoying the physical aspect of their relationship, they didn't do as much talking as they used to. She was beginning to realise that sort of intimacy was as important to her as the sex. Ewen's hurry to leave was making her think he didn't feel the same.

'Yeah, but it's probably for the best that we keep to separate rooms. We don't want to fall into something that neither of us is ready for.'

'No, of course not.' Bonnie swallowed down the sudden swell of nausea, knowing she was already in deeper than she'd intended.

Though she was enjoying her job and her freedom, the highlight of her days was getting to spend time with Ewen. She was falling for him. It wasn't something she'd expected, or wanted, but it had happened nonetheless. Ewen had shown her how being with someone could be fun and exciting, without having to live in constant fear. She hadn't expected to want another relationship with someone, but spending time with Ewen made her think about exploring the possibility. He was clearly still wary after being hurt by his ex, but she hoped that some day he might start to lower his defences too. Then they might have a chance at something even more special.

As long as she didn't scare him off in the meantime.

'I guess I'll see you around.' Ewen paused to give her a brief kiss on the lips.

Clutching the bed covers to cover her nakedness when her emotions were making her feel vulnerable, she offered him a bright smile as he left. Pretending that being a convenient lay was enough for now. Though her body was satisfied, the rest of her was decidedly antsy. She'd grown close to Ewen and was beginning to think she was ready for more than a casual arrangement.

If Ewen didn't come to feel the same way, her whole world could be in jeopardy once again.

Ewen threw himself down on top of his bed, not bothering to undress again. He hadn't been able to get out of Bonnie's room quick enough. The sound of his heavy breathing filling the dark room was only partly to do with his physical exertions. It was fear that had his heart beating so fast he thought it might explode.

He'd done his best to keep his emotions at bay around Bonnie. Convinced himself that having a purely physical relationship would protect him. So why had it been on the tip of his tongue to tell her that he had feelings for her?

He could put it down to the euphoria of the moment. Making love to Bonnie made him feel like the king of the world, there was nothing on earth like it. Therein lay the problem. It wasn't just sex any more. As much as he'd tried to keep their encounters passionate, with no room to discuss those deeply personal matters that had brought them so close in the first place, it was all to no avail.

In those moments when he wasn't kissing her, touching her, or sharing her bed, he was thinking about her. He was invested in her. That was why he'd had to leave her tonight. Before he confessed his feelings, his want for something more than a fling. Because that went against everything he'd been trying to do to protect his heart.

He couldn't leave himself exposed like that. Waiting for her to reject him and abandon him like his family, like Victoria. This was a transition stage for Bonnie. She'd just come out of an abusive relationship and the timing certainly wasn't ideal for either of them to enter a serious commitment. He could take a chance, but he knew what he felt for Bonnie was so strong already that it would kill him if she rejected him too.

As always, Ewen's response when things got complicated was to retreat somewhere alone to deal with his feelings. He had a lot to think about and he could only do that with a clear head, away from Bonnie.

'Can I have a selection of the orange blossom and dark chocolate ones and…some praline swirls?'

'Of course.' Bonnie waited as the customer

perused the glass case, making the crucial decision about which chocolates she wanted.

'I might take a few back for my husband too...'

It always took people a while to choose when there was such a wide range, but it was Bonnie's favourite part of her job. Watching people enthuse over her work, mouths watering, eyes wide, like children on Christmas morning not knowing which present to open first. Despite losing out on a childhood to follow in her father's footsteps, she was glad now to have a skill she was able to fall back on.

Bonnie carefully dropped the chocolates into the gift box with her tongs and sealed it with a sticker emblazoned with an image of the castle. Branding that made her products exclusive to castle visitors, and a tasty souvenir of their visit. Something she hoped to make available to a wider demographic at some stage. Her past had made her wary of getting too optimistic about the future, but with her new job, and Ewen in her life, she had a lot to look forward to.

Nights with Ewen were wonderful. Being in his arms, not having to go too far to get to work at a job she loved, was everything she could have wanted. However, experience had taught her things weren't always what they seemed at first. Not to take things at face value. Handsome, successful Ewen might appear to be the perfect man, certainly everything she needed at the moment, but he had his own emotional baggage. The last thing she needed was to get involved in anyone else's drama when she'd just escaped her own. As long as they kept things low-key, and they didn't get carried away with the idea of romance, things might be okay. After all, it hadn't worked out for either of them in the past.

'Thank you so much.' She took payment from her customer and handed over the bag of goodies, just as another group of excited elderly ladies walked in.

It was good to keep busy, so her thoughts weren't fully occupied with Ewen. Her new life shouldn't revolve around one man. She'd learned that lesson the hard way.

'I have a few free samples here, ladies, if you'd like to try before you buy.' Bonnie walked out from behind the counter with a tray, knowing no one could resist free chocolate.

A chorus of 'oohs' filled the little shop as she passed through the queue.

'Did you make these yourself?' one curious woman asked as she inspected a milk chocolate, caramel parcel, probably looking for flaws.

'Yes. All made in the castle kitchen by my own fair hands.' Strictly speaking it was the café kitchen, but people liked the romance.

'What flavour is this one?' another of the ladies asked after popping a whole truffle in her mouth.

'That's a Black Forest truffle. These ones are red velvet, and we have a cappuccino-flavoured one for the coffee lovers.'

The prospective customer turned her nose up at that one, then proceeded to help herself to each of the others. Bonnie had a feeling this was going to be one of those times when they treated it like a buffet rather than a sample, so she'd be left holding an empty tray. It ate into her day's profits when people got greedy, but she couldn't say anything or she ran the risk of losing a sale, so she had to grin and bear it. She could always whip up some more during that quiet period between lunchtime and closing.

'Do you have any more of those white-chocolate, whisky ones?' A familiar voice sounded from the doorway, and her heart gave that extra kick at the sight of Ewen. Even when her head was telling her not to read too much into their new dynamic, her body betrayed her true feelings.

'I always save some specially for you, Your Grace. Ladies, this is our very own duke.' She set the sample tray down on top of the counter and went in search of the whisky-flavoured truffles he was so partial to. Leaving Ewen to be mobbed by some excited tourists.

'Morning,' he said, shooting daggers at her over the top of their heads.

Bonnie blew him a kiss and grabbed a bag of whisky truffles.

'Ooh, can I get some of those too?'

'Me too.'

'My husband would love those.'

Attention shifted to the small bag of chocolates now in Ewen's possession. They obviously thought this was some sort of under-the-counter, only-for-the-duke, secret stash. Bonnie didn't have the heart to tell them she just hadn't restocked the display yet.

Ewen took a seat at the back of the shop and waited whilst she parcelled up the rest of her whisky-flavoured stock. She didn't know what had brought him here, but he clearly wanted to talk, since he was willing to give up part of his working day to wait for her. Once all the purchases were complete, and the ladies had said goodbye to her, and their new favourite duke, Ewen came up to the counter.

'Business been good today, then?' There was something in his demeanour that had definitely changed since she'd last seen him. He was stiff, and awkward, and acting more like a boss than someone she'd shared her bed with last night.

'Yes, it's been pretty steady.'

'I've decided to go ahead with the annual ball,'

he said, out of nowhere, taking her completely by surprise.

'That's great news! I'm sure Mrs McKenzie is delighted. What convinced you to go ahead with it?' The news gave her a little buzz of excitement. If he was planning to continue the tradition, it said that he was beginning to settle into his role here at the castle, adding to her security too. There was also the anticipation of being in attendance, of getting to dress up and dance and live out the fantasy of life at the castle.

She could just imagine Ewen in a tux waltzing her around the floor, her fabulous chiffon gown swishing around her strappy heels. It was a fairy tale come true, and she didn't even have to run to catch her pumpkin coach home before midnight. As long as she didn't expect her happy ever after with the handsome prince, it should be a perfect night.

Ewen dropped his gaze to his feet. 'I thought it was the right thing to do. I want to honour my father, my family, and my new position. It's what he would've wanted. I, er, also think it's about time I focused on the reason I'm here.'

When he eventually looked up at her again through lowered lashes, his shoulders slumped with resignation, she had a feeling she wasn't going to like what he had to say next.

'I thought things were going well? The wedding was a success and visitors are coming back to the castle. What's the problem?' She was aware the sharpness in her tone matched the defensive body language as she folded her arms, but her defence mechanism kicked in quicker these days.

'There's no problem. I just… I don't want to get distracted. We had a good time, but I don't think we should mix business and pleasure any more.'

Bonnie's stomach plummeted into the floor. So much for her lovely new life. A lot of her happiness was wrapped up in him, and the expectation of spending her nights with him. She'd invested her heart in him, in them, when clearly Ewen hadn't.

'You don't want to see me again?' She hated how small and pitiful her voice sounded, but this felt more brutal than anything her ex had inflicted on her. Maybe because she cared about him, wanted to be with him, it hurt so much more.

'I'll still see you every day.' He gave her a half-smile, which only made her sadder. 'It could never have been anything serious anyway, so it's probably for the best that we end things now before anyone gets hurt.'

'Sure.' She plastered on a bright smile for his benefit, and to preserve the last dregs of her self-respect.

In that moment it didn't matter that he was right, that if they let things go on the way they were she'd only fall harder, deeper, for him. All that mattered was the loss she was already experiencing.

It was then she decided she really needed to work on those defences more. She'd only just left one damaging relationship and she was already hurting again. So she steeled herself, hardened her heart, and tilted her chin in the air.

'Is that all you wanted? Because I have some whisky truffles to make.'

Ewen flinched as though she'd actually hit him, but if all he wanted was a working relationship, then that was what he would get. She wasn't about to jeopardise her home and her job if he thought she was going to make things difficult around here. It would be better for both of them if she acted as though their time together hadn't meant anything to her either.

'Okay, then. I should probably go and help Mrs McKenzie with this guest list. We've only got a few weeks to get ready and I'm going to need that time to brush up on my dancing skills.' His attempt at a joke fell flat without an engaged audience. Bonnie simply didn't have the energy to fake laugh when she'd effectively just been dumped.

'Are staff permitted to attend?' That would be

the cherry on the cake if she wasn't allowed to take part in the festivities, forced to watch from the sidelines like an unwanted wife locked in the attic. She at least wanted the dressing-up part to look forward to. There hadn't been much call for glamming up in the refuge, or any money to do it. Once she got paid, she was treating herself to a haircut and a shopping trip.

'Of course.' He looked wounded that she'd even asked, but clearly she didn't know what went on in that head when she'd thought they were going to be spending another night of passion together. Not reverting to mere work colleagues, avoiding each other as much as humanly possible.

'In that case, I'll see you there.' She turned her back on him and walked back into her kitchen. The one place she did have control. The only place she needed to be.

Today's development was going to take the shine off the fairy-tale ball, but she had to remember why she was here. It wasn't to jump into another relationship, or tie herself to another man. Especially her boss, who had the ultimate power over her, when she was only living and working here because he'd allowed it.

From now on she was going to concentrate on her position at the castle too. Everything that had happened between her and Ewen would have to

remain nothing more than a passionate inter-
lude. A reintroduction into the real world, which
would hopefully set her up for the future now
she knew she didn't have to fear every man who
crossed her path. That sex could be fun, mutu-
ally enjoyable for both participants. As long as
she didn't let emotions get in the way.

CHAPTER NINE

'WELCOME. IT'S so good to see you. Thank you for coming. Yes, it is a shame about my father, but I hope I can do him proud this evening.' Ewen greeted everyone as they came in with a clammy handshake.

Although he could legitimately call the castle his home, and he'd invited all these people here, there was still an element of unease that wouldn't let him enjoy the night. He had a lot to prove to these people, who only knew part of the story between him and his parents. His father might have apologised in a letter to him, but he certainly hadn't made the admission of his mistakes public or accepted his responsibility for their estrangement. Most of these people likely saw Ewen as the problem child who'd left his ailing father to die alone, and simply waltzed back to claim the inheritance. There were always two sides to a story, but most people were only too happy to believe the one they heard first, not interested in the backstory. Grief wasn't as sexy as the scandal of a rebellious son who killed his brother in a crash and ran away from home.

Tonight was hopefully his chance to prove he could fill his father's shoes, and that he wasn't some bad seed who was going to blow the family fortune. He'd certainly been putting all of his time and effort into making this a success tonight. Not that it was all for the benefit of others. He'd needed tasks to fill his days with something other than yearning after Bonnie and wondering what could have been.

This past month had been torturous in so many ways, seeing her every day and pretending that his feelings for her had never happened. They were civil and professional towards one another, but in a way that was almost as devastating as if she had walked away from him altogether. He'd lost a friend and a confidante, as well as a lover.

During the long, lonely nights lying awake in his room his mind was thoroughly made up about selling the castle and moving on. Then he'd see Bonnie happy in her shop and yearn to have her back in his arms. When he had her beside him this place felt more like home than it ever had. He was conflicted over his plans for the future, and, left alone to brood, he'd read and reread the letter his father had left him.

Ewen had been so engrossed in what had happened between him and Bonnie that he hadn't fully processed the contents of the note. Now he'd analysed it in greater detail, his father's words had given him a new perspective on life at BenCrag. Past and present.

His father had wanted to renew their relationship, but that same fear of rejection Ewen suffered from had prevented him from doing so. Causing them both unnecessary pain. Ewen wondered if he was making the same mistake with Bonnie. If he was hurting himself by not being with her, instead of taking that leap of faith and telling her how he really felt. He didn't want to spend the rest of his life with regrets like his old man.

Now all he had to do was get Bonnie alone and find the courage to open up. Not an easy task on the biggest night of the castle's year.

Mrs McKenzie sidled up to him, wearing a blue and green dress made from her family tartan, a brighter alternative to her usual dull tweeds. The smile was new too. 'It's so wonderful to see the castle coming alive again, isn't it?'

Ewen was tempted to remind her they'd had visitors coming for weeks now, not to mention the wedding that had taken over the castle and its grounds. But he didn't want to rain on her parade when he knew how much this meant to her. It was a reminder of the old days, and happier

times. The only difference was the duke holding
the event. He didn't know how she would cope
if he did leave and all ties to the family were
severed. Depending on what happened tonight,
this could be the last ball in the castle. Though
he couldn't even tell her that. He could only try
and make it as memorable as possible for all involved.

'I hope you've got your dancing shoes on, Mrs
McKenzie. I have you pencilled in for a reel.'

She lifted her skirt and turned her ankle,
showing off a pair of sturdy heels. 'I'm looking
forward to it.'

A couple came through the doors that she
seemed to recognise, and she left Ewen greeting the guests at the door to go with them into
the main hall where the dance was being held.

Everyone was in their finery, the event an excuse for people to dress up and enjoy themselves.
He could see why it was a highly anticipated day
on the calendar. Regardless that the decision to
hold it had been last minute, all the RSVPs had
come in thick and fast. It seemed the regular attendees had kept their diaries open just in case,
and for that he was thankful. It wouldn't have
been quite the same if it had been only him and
the castle staff in attendance.

He glanced back at the familiar group banded
together at the back of the room, clutching their

drinks and chatting among themselves. Specifically letting his gaze fall on Bonnie, who looked amazing.

She'd really gone all out tonight, her hair cascading onto her shoulders in soft chocolate waves, her smoky eye make-up and the slick of crimson lipstick highlighting all her best features. Along with the off-the-shoulder, slinky satin red dress, with the train at the back skimming the floor. It clung to her full breasts, the indent at her waist, and her curvy hips. The epitome of a siren, calling to every man in the room who couldn't take his eyes off her. Including Ewen. Though he didn't even try to fool himself that this was for his benefit, when she'd been brusque with him on the occasions that they had interacted.

She'd taken to having her breakfast half an hour earlier than he did, eating dinner in the shop at night, so they didn't have to make awkward small talk in the castle kitchen. It was what he had asked for, space to concentrate on events at the castle. Except numerous phone calls, meetings with suppliers and auditioning ceilidh bands hadn't managed to take his mind off her.

Seeing her tonight wasn't going to help with that. Every part of the castle seemed to have her imprinted on it. The kitchen, his apartment, the stairs…now even the ballroom. He missed her. It had been his idea to call things off before they had a chance to begin, but he'd spent just as much time thinking about her as if he'd simply let things play out. The only difference was that he was miserable inside because he couldn't be with her. He'd be lucky if she'd even give him five minutes of her time tonight.

'Aren't you coming in, Your Grace? The dance is about to start.' One of the volunteers who helped with the gardens, a horticulture student from the local college, touched him lightly on the arm.

She was the last to arrive, windswept and alone, and clearly a little anxious about walking into the party on her own.

'In that case, may I escort you inside, Sara? I think I saw some of your friends in there.' He angled his arm and offered it to her in support, though he was glad he wasn't walking in solo either. The idea of having to succeed, of making a good impression on his father's friends and acquaintances, was a lot of pressure. Part of the reason he'd invited the junior members of staff too, young enough not to hold a grudge against him.

'Thank you, Your Grace,' she said, slipping her arm into his and clinging on for dear life.

'Just call me Ewen.' He grimaced every time someone addressed him according to his status.

It reminded him of his father, and wasn't a title he was sure he lived up to yet.

The other guests were milling around the room, enjoying the glasses of champagne and drams of whisky being passed round by the waiting staff. Everyone was dressed in brightly coloured gowns and tartans, but his eyes automatically went to the flash of red in the corner. She was talking to Richard, the estate manager. The handsome, *single* estate manager, who currently had his hand on Bonnie's arm.

Ewen found himself steering Sara towards them, enjoying the flash of irritation in Bonnie's eyes.

'Good evening. Richard, Bonnie, this is Sara, she's one of our gardening volunteers.'

'Hi, yes, I think you bought some of my dark chocolate lavender creams the other day.' Bonnie offered her a welcoming smile in stark contrast to the dark look he'd received upon his approach.

'They were a present for my granny and she loved them. I think I'll have a standing order now.' Sara laughed.

'Nice to see you again, Sara. We met when we were landscaping that overgrown land behind the old stables,' Richard explained to Ewen and Bonnie.

'Yes, how is that coming?' Sara enquired,

dropping her arm from Ewen's, her attention now on Richard.

'I have some pictures on my phone if you'd like to see. You should stop by next time you're here. I'd like to get some new eyes on the project.' Richard pulled out his phone to show Sara what he'd been working on, and the couple drifted away from Bonnie and Ewen.

'You look amazing,' he told her, unable to ignore the obvious now his buffer had disappeared.

'Thank you. You've done a great job putting all of this together,' she said, gesturing around the room.

'Well, Mrs McKenzie had a lot of input, but I'm happy with the turnout.' His main worry had been that no one would show up, unwilling to give him a chance, like so many people in his life. But he'd underestimated the enthusiasm for the annual event. He had Mrs McKenzie to thank for persuading him to go ahead, otherwise he might never have won people over.

An uneasy silence descended between them, highlighted even more by the chatter going on in the room around them. He hated this new awkward dynamic when they'd been so close at the beginning. As close as two people could be. That was probably why he'd backed away, afraid things would develop into something more serious than he'd anticipated. Those wounds Victoria and his parents had left upon him preventing him from even taking a chance. Afraid of further rejection and heartbreak. Of being left alone again.

However, as he'd found, it wasn't as easy to simply shut off those emotions and forget how she'd made him feel. Why else had he barrelled straight over at the sight of her talking to another man? A possessive move he knew would horrify her, and only made him despise himself more. It was no one else's fault but his if she did move on with someone else.

'How've you been?'

'Do you have any other events planned?'

They stumbled over each other's words, adding to the pain in his heart. They couldn't even be around one another now without things being awkward, and that wasn't going to improve the longer they dodged around each other both inside and outside work. It was probably only a matter of time before she decided to move into her own place where she was free to come and go as she pleased without fear of running into an ex. A scenario that should have suited him too, not having to be reminded of what he'd thrown away at every turn, but which also saddened him. He didn't want to imagine living in the castle on his own again.

They exchanged embarrassed half-smiles.

'I'm good. Busy getting the website up and running. Thank you for agreeing to that, by the way. I've already got some custom orders coming in, so plenty of work ahead.'

'It wasn't a problem simply adding a link on the castle main page. I'm glad you're getting some interest. You deserve it.'

'Thanks. I trust you've more events planned, since they seem to be such a success.' She probed into the castle's future again, but Ewen didn't want to look too far ahead. At least not beyond the things his father had pencilled in for the rest of the year.

'I think we've got a few craft-fair weekends planned out in the grounds, weather permitting, and maybe a New Year's bash if this goes well.'

'Hogmanay, at the castle. That sounds like a definite winner.' Her smile lit up the dark corner of the room, but also squeezed his heart like a vice. Not only because he missed her, but also because he wasn't sure if he'd still be in the castle beyond Hogmanay.

'Ladies and gentlemen. Dinner will now be served in the main dining room, if you'd care to make your way there.'

Before Ewen cracked and told her how much he was missing her, dinner was announced, and all the attendees began to file out.

'Shall we?' He held out his arm to escort Bonnie to the dining room. Hoping it wouldn't be the last time he'd get to touch her.

The whole scene was something Bonnie had never dreamed she could ever be part of, chandeliers sparkling from the arched, ornamental ceilings making everything look so much more magical. Her heart was beating frantically with every step they took, but she was glad Ewen had taken it upon himself to escort her to dinner. Even if it was merely out of politeness.

She missed his touch, missed being with him. It was difficult living and working in the same place, unable to escape the memories or feelings associated with him. She'd have to find her own place soon, before he started seeing someone else and completely broke her heart.

'It's all right. I've got you,' Ewen whispered, sensing her unease as they walked into the dining room. As always, doing his best to take care of her feelings.

It was daunting being in a room full of people, most of whom she didn't know. Especially when she was dressed the way she was tonight. At first, the idea of glamming up had been thrilling, something she'd looked forward to. The shine somewhat wearing off when Ewen had called a halt to their fling so early on. With a little time to herself, she'd decided it was a chance for her to dress the way she wanted for once.

After years of being told what she couldn't wear, of not being able to look how she wanted, she'd gone a bit mad with power. Now she wondered if the vamp look had been overkill, and if it had been to get Ewen's attention. Either way it appeared to have worked. Okay, so she had wanted him to see what he was missing, but he looked better than ever too in his formal tight-fitting tux jacket and kilt.

The weeks since their night together had been lonely. Though she'd proved to herself, and everyone else, she was more than capable of looking after herself, it had been nice to have his company. Nicer still to share a bed with someone who took care of her needs as well as their own.

Being with him had been the happiest time of her life. Ewen had shown her she was capable of having a normal relationship, that she didn't have to settle for someone who treated her badly. She'd stopped flinching every time someone raised their voice, enjoyed being touched without wondering when it would turn to something violent. Thanks to Ewen she could be comfortable around men again. But there was only one she wanted. It was a shame he couldn't give her the serious commitment she knew she wanted now.

She'd liked being in a relationship, even for a

little while. Enjoyed having someone to spend her evenings with, to talk with about her day over a shared meal. But she wanted a partner who wasn't afraid to show his emotions. Who didn't freak out at the thought of spending the night with her. She deserved someone who would love her completely, and apparently that wasn't Ewen.

'I think that's your seat there.' Ewen unhooked her arm and led her to her name card on the vast banqueting table laid with shining cutlery and crystal-clear glasses.

'Thank you.' She took her seat and watched as he walked down to take his seat at the end of the table.

It would have been easier for her to have him sitting beside her, regardless of their current awkwardness, rather than the two strangers who sat down either side of her. She consoled herself that at least he was still in her eyeline, close enough that she could hear him, giving her some sense of familiarity in the situation.

'You're a new face around here.' A deep voice sounded from the seat next to her.

She turned to find an elderly, distinguished gentleman peering at her through horn rimmed spectacles.

'I just moved here. I run the chocolate shop in the castle.'

Her dinner companion frowned, and she wondered if he was the type who thought the hired help shouldn't be dining at the table. 'Are you the lass that made the chocolate castle? I was a guest at the wedding here last month. Incredible work.'

Bonnie let out a sigh of relief. 'Yes, that was me. Thank you.'

It was always nice to get positive feedback on her work, and she hoped the little treats she'd made to give out to the guests at the end of the evening would earn her more future custom too.

'It's good to have some new blood at the castle. It would be a shame if it fell into more commercial hands, and it lost the local charm. I knew the late duke…a terrible loss to the community.'

'So I understand. I never actually met him, but he was very kind in taking me on.' She had him to thank for everything.

'What do you think of the son? He's a new face around here too.' The gentleman sniffed.

Bonnie was uncomfortable engaging in any negative conversation involving Ewen when her personal feelings were so wrapped up in him and everything at the castle. She couldn't bear to hear anyone talk ill of him either, when they didn't know the full, painful family history. So she tried to be as diplomatic as possible.

'Ewen is doing his best to honour his father's legacy under some very difficult circumstances.'

'Yes, I understand there was some bad blood between them after the eldest was killed. A car crash, I understand.'

'An accident, which I think left the whole family grieving. I think he was very brave to come back and pick up where his father left off.' She had to defend him when she knew what had gone on behind the scenes to get him to this place. Ewen would never make the contents of his father's letter public, which would have exonerated him of any wrongdoing, because he was too proud, and protective of the family name. He wouldn't want to air the family's dirty washing in public.

Ewen was a man of honour. A hard worker who tried to do the right thing by everyone. Not to mention amazing in bed. Okay, so that might have coloured her view a little, and was information she wouldn't be sharing either, but it didn't take away from the fact he was just a wonderful person.

'He has big shoes to fill, but, if tonight is anything to go by, I think the community will welcome him back with open arms.' The gentleman toasted the new duke with his dram of whisky before taking a sip, and Bonnie was relieved Ewen was beginning to win people over. He deserved his place here, and she knew he'd work hard to do what was best for the castle, and the people employed there. Including her.

The sound of his laughter from the head of the table caught her attention. He was laughing at something the woman on his right had said. Bonnie slowly zoned out from the conversation she'd been in to try and hear what had amused Ewen. She was experiencing the same irrational envy now as she had when he'd walked in with the pretty young blonde earlier, regardless that they obviously weren't together.

It was that want to be the woman making him laugh, to be with him, that made her realise she'd fallen for him. Given that they hadn't been to-gether for weeks, the damage had clearly already been done. Now she was doomed to watch him from the sidelines as he captivated other women. She wasn't looking forward to meeting his next conquest over the breakfast table.

Ewen caught her eye and gave her a heart-racing smile. A private moment just between the two of them in this room full of strangers that made her wish they were alone. That he'd never ended the best thing to happen to her in years.

Ewen took a swig of whisky to steady his nerves before he got to his feet. He didn't think he'd get heckled at his own dinner, but that didn't make it any easier to stand in front of his father's friends and acquaintances and make a speech.

'Ladies and gentlemen, could I have your attention, please?' He waited until the hubbub of conversation subsided. 'Thank you.'

'You've had my attention all night,' one of the more inebriated female guests shouted to make him blush. The interruption raised a few titters around the table and broke the ice for him.

Ewen glanced over at Bonnie, who was sitting tight-lipped, glaring daggers at the new member of his fan club. It made him smile that she should be outraged on his behalf, or might even have been touched by the green-eyed monster at the thought that someone else should be interested in him. Perhaps he hadn't completely ruined things with Bonnie. She hadn't flinched when he'd offered to escort her to dinner, and had almost looked disappointed when she'd found she wasn't sitting with him. His pulse picked up along with his spirits. All might not be lost after all.

Deciding to ignore the vocal adulation, Ewen cleared his throat and continued. 'I just wanted to take this opportunity to thank you all for coming tonight. It's been a difficult time for everyone who knew my father, and an upheaval for those working at the castle.'

He gave a nod to all the staff currently seated, grateful that they'd all stayed on to help him keep the place running. 'I'd have been lost these past weeks if you hadn't all pitched in to show me the ropes, so thank you.'

He raised his glass and toasted his new friends to a chorus of approval from the rest of the guests.

'Anyway, tonight is about honouring my father, and he would want us all to eat, drink, and dance the night away. So if you'd care to raise your glasses, I'd like to make a toast to my father, the duke.'

'The duke.' The room echoed with the sentiment and Ewen found himself becoming choked up.

As always when he was struggling, feelings of grief and remorse overwhelming him, he sought out Bonnie to centre him. Her eyes were glistening with tears as she gave him a wobbly smile and raised her glass to him. Ewen knew it wasn't just his father she was toasting and he wanted to hold her in his arms more than ever.

Before he could go too far down that rabbit hole, the sound of the band filtered through the air. The upbeat tempo of traditional Scottish folk music immediately altered the mood of the place, and he was grateful for it. He would've hated to be responsible for a maudlin atmosphere at what was supposed to be the highlight of the year in the village.

'It sounds as though the party's starting without us, so if you'd all like to make your way back to the main hall, we'll get our dancing shoes on.' He gave everyone permission to leave, and took a minute for himself, watching as everyone headed out of the room. With one notable exception.

Bonnie hung back until everyone had left before moving towards Ewen. 'I know that couldn't have been easy for you, but you did a good job. Of everything. Your father would've been proud.'

Ewen didn't realise how much he'd needed to hear that, how much he needed Bonnie, until she hugged him. It was a brief, empathetic reaction to something she knew was an emotional matter for him, but it was the contact he'd been yearning for. He didn't want the night to end, didn't want to go back to the real world, avoiding each other at work because it was too painful otherwise.

'Thanks. I suppose I should really go in there and start shaking my stuff.' He deployed some humour to try and defuse the situation.

Bonnie made a *tsk* sound. 'I'm not sure you'll want to do that. I think that might be enough to start a stampede of drunk cougars headed your way.'

Ewen loved the tinge of jealousy he swore he heard in her voice as they made their way towards the sounds of the ceilidh. It proved she still cared.

The dancing was already under way, and as they entered the room Ewen could feel all the men stand up a little straighter. All eyes on Bonnie. He wasn't ready to let her go again.

'May I have this dance?' he asked with a bow and his hand extended towards her.

'I'm not sure I'd make a good partner. I haven't danced in a long time.' She hesitated, but he was sure it was due to her lack of experience rather than who was asking.

'Perfect! Neither have I.' It would be expected of him to take part, and he knew he'd feel much more comfortable in the spotlight if Bonnie was with him. Although he wouldn't push it if she really didn't want to accompany him onto the dance floor.

Given her history, he would never force her to do anything she didn't want, and he hoped she understood that.

He was about to leave, resigning himself to making a show of himself solo, when she threw her hands up in the air.

'Sod it. You only live once, right? You were brave enough to go ahead with this tonight, so I'm sure I can cope with making a fool of myself on the dance floor.' She took his hand and walked forward, chin held high.

Ewen was proud of her. This was a woman who'd been through serious trauma, who would have had every right to hide away from the world. But that wasn't Bonnie. Instead, she was throwing herself out there, being the true version of herself—strong and beautiful. An amazing woman he couldn't believe he'd almost let slip through his fingers.

They joined the throng on the floor, who'd already arranged themselves into two lines facing one another. Ewen and Bonnie broke into the lines, holding hands with their fellow dancers and asking each other what they'd got themselves into. Luckily there was a caller to remind them of the dance moves.

After a short countdown, the dancing couples advanced towards one another, then retreated. Ewen and Bonnie were lagging behind a little trying to keep up with what was happening.

They split into parties of four, hands in the middle, spinning around one way, then the other.

'Now, do-si-do!'

Following the caller's instruction, and the others around them, Ewen and Bonnie passed each other back-to-back, arms folded. They weren't slick, or co-ordinated, but neither was anyone else, the free bar obviously having an effect on the quality of dancing. But everyone was having fun, and the sound of Bonnie's laughter made everything worthwhile.

'I think I need a drink,' he shouted over the music once the dance had ended, a tad out of breath.

'Just one more dance,' Bonnie begged, tugging him back onto the floor.

How could he refuse when she looked so happy, and it was another chance to be close to her?

They linked arms and spun around with the rest of the guests. Clapped and whooped, and skipped the length and breadth of the hall until they were both red-faced and out of breath. For more than one dance. When it finally came to a gentle waltz, Ewen took Bonnie into his arms with some relief. Neither of them had hesitated to partner up with each other for the slow dance. He took it as a positive sign that she didn't hate the sight of him altogether, since she'd been content to dance with him for most of the evening.

'Have you enjoyed yourself tonight?'

'I have. I was worried about socialising with so many people I don't know. I've been a bit isolated these past few years.'

Even though her grin said she was joking, Ewen knew it was also something of an understatement. From everything she'd told him she'd practically been a prisoner in her own home.

He could only imagine how overwhelming this could have been if she hadn't confronted it so head-on. Even he'd had sleepless nights over having a bunch of strangers in his home, judging him and his actions, and he was used to the bustling streets of London until recently. For Bonnie to be such a part of his big night meant a lot to him, and spoke volumes about the special kind of person she was. The sort of woman he should've snapped up when he had the chance.

'I miss you.' The words fell from his lips into her ear as they slow-danced around the floor.

Bonnie stiffened in his arms and he immediately regretted opening his mouth.

'Sorry. That wasn't fair of me. Forget I said anything.'

She locked her eyes onto his. 'It was your idea to call things off. Not mine.'

'I know, and I've been kicking myself every day since.' That bud of hope threatened to fully bloom when she reminded him that she'd been happy with the set-up. It opened up the possibility that she would be willing to give him another chance.

At least in his head.

'What is it you want from me, Ewen?' Bonnie didn't know if the ache in her heart was from false hope or fear she was giving him an opportunity to hurt her all over again by even entertaining whatever he had to say to her.

They'd spent most of the evening together. Something she hadn't planned, but had enjoyed nonetheless. When he said things like he was missing her, it only set her up for more heartbreak if nothing more was going to come of it. It was only when he'd called things off that she'd realised the true depth of her feelings for Ewen. Knowing if he'd expressed an interest in making things serious, she would've been prepared to risk her heart on him. Except he'd ended things instead.

She'd missed him every minute of every day, but had to get on with things as best she could, because that was what she did. What she'd been doing for years. And she was afraid to expect more.

'I don't know,' he said honestly, which didn't do anything to help her. 'I just know I want you back in my life as more than a member of staff who's constantly trying to avoid me.'

His smile was heartbreaking. She'd taken steps to protect herself, eating at different times so she didn't have to see him all the time and be reminded of their nights together. It hadn't occurred to her that it might be hurting him just as much.

'We're leaving. I just wanted to thank you for

such a wonderful evening. Looking forward to the next one.' A tall, well-dressed man tapped Ewen on the shoulder to get his attention, interrupting his heart-to-heart with Bonnie.

He gave her a look of apology, but she understood he couldn't ignore his guests. They broke hold so he could shake hands with the man, and his partner.

'Thanks for coming. I'll see you out.' He turned back to mouth an apology to Bonnie and she nodded an 'okay' in response. It was part of his duty as host, she knew it was nothing personal when he'd been keen to talk to her.

Bonnie moved to a seat at the side of the room, glad to take off her shoes and rest after the earlier energetic dancing. She saw little more of Ewen as more and more couples took their leave. Every time he appeared at the door, someone else was keen to say their goodbyes and shake hands with the now popular duke. Whatever preconceptions they'd had about him had obviously been put to rest over the course of the night, and she was pleased he'd achieved his objective, along with honouring his father's memory.

It showed a lot of restraint, and social etiquette, that he hadn't felt the need to explain himself, to lay the blame for his estrangement from the family at his parents' feet, when they'd treated him so appallingly. She wasn't sure she would've been so magnanimous in the circumstances. Although she was in similar circumstances with her own mother and father, she knew she had to shoulder some of the blame for her actions. They'd just been trying to protect her. Even if they'd gone about it the wrong way. If they had as many regrets about their actions as she did, she thought it might be worth trying to salvage a relationship before it was too late and she was left in the same emotional turmoil as Ewen appeared to be in.

Bonnie watched as the room gradually emptied. The band packed up their instruments, the lights came back on, and it began to feel as though she'd been stood up on a date, people looking at her with pity. In the end, weary and wanting to hold onto a shred of dignity, she decided to go to bed. If Ewen really wanted to speak to her he could find her. He knew where she worked and lived. She'd spent enough of her life being dangled like a puppet on a man's whim.

On her way up the stairs to her room she noticed the door was ajar. Ewen was outside holding court and laughing with a group of revellers. She didn't begrudge him the chance to make new friends and acquaintances, or enjoy his new status, having charmed everyone in the village. However, it was a reminder she wasn't a priority in his life. Something he'd made clear the last time they'd been together. She was only worthy of a casual fling, nothing more serious. And, whilst it had been by mutual agreement at the time, now she realised she deserved more.

If she was going to share her life with another man, it had to be someone who treated her feelings as a priority, not an afterthought. What these past weeks had shown her was that she was more than capable of taking care of herself, so why should she open herself up to someone who thought he could pick her up and set her down when he chose?

She stomped her way back to her room as much as her bare feet would allow, stripped off her dress, wiped off her make-up, and put on her comfy pyjamas. The knock on her door didn't come as a complete surprise, and she realised her quick change had been out of defiance. If she hadn't been enough to capture his attention in all her finery, she was done making the effort.

'I'm sorry. I'm sorry. I'm sorry,' he said when she opened the door.

She cocked an eyebrow at him and folded her arms across her chest. 'I know you didn't expect me to sit around like some love-struck school-girl waiting on you all night.'

'Of course not. I really wanted to talk to you. It's just…people wanted to chat, to share memories of my dad and the nights they used to have here at the castle. I didn't want to be rude and walk away, but I am sorry I let you down.' The sincere remorse was evident in the slump of his shoulders, and the puppy-dog eyes begging for forgiveness made her wilt.

'It's okay,' she relented, remembering that this whole thing had been about remembering his father, not her love life.

'Trust me, I would much rather have been spending that time with you. You looked amazing tonight.' He was leaning against the door jamb, his voice seeming to drop an octave as his eyes swept over her. Making her feel as though she were still wearing her sexy red dress and heels, not her fleecy, sloth-covered pjs.

Her heart started that dangerous arrythmia that followed every time he looked at her. More apparent now they were alone and he wasn't even trying to disguise the fact he found her attractive.

'Sorry. I changed as soon as I got in. I thought the moment between us had passed.'

He dropped his head as though he'd been punched in the gut. 'You still look amazing, but I should've waited until everyone had gone before I tried to start that conversation. You deserve my undivided attention, Bonnie.'

The way he was looking at her, she knew she had it now.

Bonnie swallowed hard, trying not to slide into a puddle of want on her doorstep.

'So, what was it you wanted to talk about?' She did her best impression of a woman holding it together, indifferent to the man standing in front of her begging her to hear him out.

'Us.'

'There is no us. That was your decision, Ewen.' She wasn't going to let him get away from that fact lightly.

'Well, I'm not known for making the best decisions, am I?' Another flash of that endearing smile and the twinkle of his eyes ensured she would at least hear him out.

'And ending things between us was…?'

'A big mistake. Huge.' He gave her a self-deprecating grin that almost convinced her to let him off. Except she needed more convincing she wouldn't be the one full of regret if she relented now.

'Ewen, I've had time to think too, and, you know, I don't think a fling is enough for me. If I'm going to be with someone it'll be because they want to be with me, not because I'm convenient. We work together, we live together, and I just think it should be all or nothing. I'm not saying I want to get married and have babies, but

I'm saying I do want some level of commitment. I think I deserve that at least.' She didn't think it was too much to ask to have some sort of security in a relationship. Something normal, that wasn't limited to within the walls of the castle.

'You do. I know we rushed head first into things, but I would like to try again. We've both been hurt in the past, and I think we chose a casual arrangement because it felt safer. I ended it because I knew I would want more and I didn't think I was ready for that. Ready to risk my heart on someone again. Being without you these past weeks has been torture and made me realise I'd rather take that risk than not be with you at all. We can take it slow if that's what you want. If you're even willing to give me another chance...'

Bonnie scrunched her face up. 'I don't know... I think I have a few demands which need to be met before I agree to anything.'

'Your wish is my command.' He stepped farther into her room, sliding his hands around her waist, and sending her hormones into overdrive.

'Not those kinds of needs. Although... I'm sure a little sweetener would help seal the deal...' She tilted her head back as he began kissing his way along her neck, the friction of his beard against her skin making her shiver with delight.

'Tell me what you need, Bonnie.' His voice

was thick with longing, his breath hot in her ear, and her entire body seemed to ache for him.

'I want…' Bonnie fought to find words through the fog of desire currently consuming her. She closed her eyes and tried to focus on her thoughts rather than the sensations rushing through her body.

'I want to go out. To date. To be part of a couple. All the fun things I've missed out on for so long.' Any good memories she had of the early days with her ex when he'd been wooing her were now tarnished with the realisation he'd been lulling her into a false sense of security. Now she wanted the real deal.

'Done. We can go steady.' He paused his perusal of her skin with his mouth. 'Does that mean you want me to go now? To forget what we've already had and start from scratch?'

She thought about it briefly, and discovered her head and her heart differed greatly on the matter. In the end she went with the feelings she was having somewhere lower than her gut.

'No.' She grabbed him by the shirt collar and pulled him fully inside the room, kicking the door shut behind him.

There was no point pretending their time together hadn't happened. Certainly, she didn't want to. There was nothing to be gained from being coy now, and she had a lot of lost ground to make up for in the bedroom department.

'Good,' he growled, and backed her towards the bed.

Perhaps she was making it too easy for him, but this was what she wanted too, and there was no better way to get over her past than by taking control of her own wants.

Ewen was unbuttoning her pyjamas whilst he kissed her, taking his sweet time about it. The graze of his fingers travelling down her body flooding her with arousal. She was more impatient, tugging at his jacket, unbuttoning his shirt, until he got the message and pulled them off himself. His clothes quickly followed by hers as they tumbled onto her bed.

'I'm sorry it's not quite the same standard as your room,' she muttered against his lips.

'I wouldn't care if we were in the dungeon, I'd still be happy as long as I was with you,' he said, palming her breast and teasing her nipples into tight buds.

'There's a dungeon? Is that a duke kink?'

'Not yet.' Ewen playfully grabbed both of her wrists and held them above her head in one of his large hands.

It could've been a macho display of strength used to intimidate her, but she knew that wasn't Ewen. She wasn't frightened or cowed by his actions, merely turned on. Not least because, whilst she was incapacitated, he was kissing his way all over her body, driving her nuts when she couldn't touch him in return.

When he did loosen his grip, his attention diverted towards her breasts again, she took the opportunity to break free.

'Condoms. We need condoms,' she said breathlessly, pushing herself up off the bed.

'I didn't think to put any in my sporran,' Ewen said with a grin as he moved aside to let her get up.

'I have some in the bathroom cabinet. I thought when we decided to have a casual fling that we might need them.' She had no need to be embarrassed. It was the sensible thing to do. Yet she didn't want him to think there had been anyone else. She supposed the fact that he hadn't been carrying protection around with him suggested perhaps he hadn't been sleeping around either. The thought comforted her as she retrieved a foil packet from the bathroom.

When she came back into the room, Ewen was lying gorgeously naked on her bed waiting, arms behind his head, looking as though that was exactly where he was meant to be.

'What?' he asked.

'I was just thinking you look very at home. I mean, I know the castle *is* your home, but you look comfortable in my bed.' She straddled him and handed over the shiny prize.

'Not comfortable, per se, in my current state,' he joked and drew her attention to his impressive arousal. 'But I am very happy to be here.'

'So I see.' She bent down and kissed him on the mouth, reconnecting, and picking up where they'd left off.

Except something had changed between them. The earlier frenzied passion replaced with a tenderness. A new softness in the kissing that suggested this was more than just sex now. They didn't have to rush, or hide away any more. If they were embarking on a new relationship, they had all the time in the world to explore one another. Along with their feelings.

Bonnie rolled over onto her back, taking Ewen with her. She wanted to feel loved tonight, to let him take control.

'I need you, Ewen.'

He stopped kissing her long enough to check that was what she wanted. 'Are you sure?'

She arched her hips up off the bed to meet his. 'I'm sure.'

That was all the confirmation he needed as he sheathed himself and slowly filled her. Bonnie gasped, adjusting to that initial union of their bodies, and Ewen paused. Kissing her so tenderly any tension in her body immediately melted away. She wanted this, wanted him, for as long as possible.

When she'd left her ex she'd never have believed she'd want to be with anyone else again. It said a lot about Ewen that she was willing to open up her heart and her life to him so soon. She was putting all of her trust in him not to hurt her. He let her make her own choices, didn't try to exert control over her the way the other men in her life had. Although it was early days, she had a good feeling about their relationship. They'd already been through so much, she knew neither of them wanted any more drama or deceit. Hopefully they were going into an honest, easy relationship, with no nasty surprises lurking in the closet. What she saw was what she got with Ewen—a handsome, sexy, hardworking, loving man. It was a bonus that she got to see him every day, working in a place she loved.

For once, her future was bright.

CHAPTER TEN

EWEN FORCED HIS eyes open, though he had no desire to leave this cosy cocoon he and Bonnie had made under the covers. Especially when she was naked, and curved so invitingly against his body. He groaned as the rest of his body began to stir, knowing he had no time to indulge the carnal urges Bonnie had awakened so vigorously in him.

He knew the physical side of their relationship was so spectacular because it was about more than sex. They had a connection he'd never had with Victoria, who'd always remained a little aloof. Now he realised she'd been keeping secrets, with one eye on a better prospect. Perhaps had indulged in a few more dalliances than he was even aware of. Not that he cared any more. His life was here at the castle, with Bonnie. He'd made the decision to stay permanently in the early hours of the morning, when he'd wakened briefly with her in his arms with a feeling of contentment that he never wanted to lose again.

The castle had always represented a difficult past, but now he wanted to make plans for a future with Bonnie. He had the events side of the business to run, and she had the chocolate shop. Their life was here, and now they had each other it would start to feel like a real home again.

Trying his best not to disturb her, he eased himself away, and slid to the edge of the mattress.

'Where are you going? Afraid Mrs McKenzie won't approve?' she mumbled, her back still to him.

'Not at all. We're both adults, and my private life is nothing to do with the staff. At least, the rest of the staff.' He was aware their relationship might raise a few eyebrows, but if he and Bonnie were happy that was all that mattered. It had been a long time since he'd felt loved and wanted, and he wasn't about to throw that away simply because of someone else's opinion. He was done living his life afraid of what people thought about him. The only person's opinion that held any sway over him was Bonnie's, and after their night together he was pretty sure he'd made her happy. Several times.

'Then get back into bed.' She threw the covers back again and patted the empty space behind her.

'I wish I could. Trust me, I could happily spend

the rest of my life in there with you. Unfortunately, I have a business appointment this morning.' It took every last drop of his energy to refrain from climbing back into the bed and snuggling up behind her again. However, he had an appointment this morning that he'd left too late to cancel. There were decisions to be made that were going to dictate his future, and that of the castle, now he was certain of the direction he wanted both to take.

He dropped a kiss on a sleepy Bonnie's forehead, taking a mental snapshot of her lying here so he remembered exactly why he was doing this.

'Go back to sleep. I'm just going to grab a shower and change into something less comfortable than my birthday suit.' He grabbed his clothes up off the floor, separating them from Bonnie's pyjamas, which he left on the end of the bed for her.

'I happen to like your birthday suit,' she muttered into her pillow, making Ewen laugh.

'Don't worry, I'll wear it again later. Just for you.'

With his modesty covered by the bundle of clothes in his hand, he made a dash down the hall to his room, hoping it was early enough to dodge Mrs McKenzie's eagle eyes.

Whilst he still maintained his private life was

no one else's business other than his and Bonnie's, that didn't mean he was ready to face her disapproving glare. He wanted her to know they were in a committed relationship, not just bed-hopping. It would be the more mature call to talk to her, rather than let her find out for herself.

He was sure that was what he wanted now with Bonnie. A secure, committed relationship, and a future to look forward to at the castle. These last weeks, he'd been floundering to find somewhere he belonged, and a purpose in life. The castle had held so many bad memories his knee-jerk reaction had been to sell it on. Working to get the castle up and running again with Bonnie, Mrs McKenzie, and the rest of the staff had filled that void in his life. He'd found his family.

By the time he'd showered and changed, Mrs McKenzie was already buzzing around downstairs setting the place to rights.

'Good morning. A Mr Argyle has just arrived. I've shown him into the study. That's where your father held all of his business meetings. I hope that's all right?'

She met him at the bottom of the stairs. He was sure she'd been in a dilemma about whether or not to come up and wake him. Probably worried about what she might find.

'Yes, that's fine.' Although he'd been dealing with companies involved in the events side of castle business, it had mostly been over the phone. Or, in the case of the ceilidh band, over video call. He supposed he had to find his own rhythm, but it would be a shame not to utilise the space his father had carefully curated for business purposes.

Apart from anything else, he wanted the privacy. It would upset the current status quo around here if it became common knowledge that he'd considered selling the place. He didn't need that kind of discord when they'd just started working together as a team.

'Mr Argyle, it's a pleasure to meet you.' Ewen walked over to the premier estate agent he'd forgotten he'd even contacted about the sale of the castle. The slick suited and booted visitor stood to shake his hand.

'Thank you for inviting me over. It's such a wonderful opportunity for my company to be involved in a property with such history.' He reached for his briefcase and began unpacking files onto the desk. His enthusiasm making Ewen flinch.

'I'm afraid it might be something of a wasted journey.' Ewen took his seat at the desk, making sure there was some distance between them when he broke the news that there wouldn't be a mega commission coming his way after all.

'I know you said you wouldn't be selling until next year, and you just wanted me to put out a few feelers for possible interest in the property, but I couldn't help myself. I took the liberty of mocking up a brochure using some of the photographs and information available online. I think if we spark some interest now you might get a bidding war on your hands.' An enthusiastic Mr Argyle handed over a slick property brochure inside a leather binder.

Everything about this man screamed money and Ewen began to think he'd had a lucky escape. If money was his sole motivation, he might not have had the castle's best interests at heart. The staff could've found themselves unemployed, with their workplace sold on to property developers for a pretty penny. There was enough land on the property to build an entire new housing development. Ewen doubted this man, or his contacts, would've had any interest in the history of the castle, or the people who lived and worked there.

He couldn't imagine the beautiful surroundings he'd grown up in being bulldozed to throw up high-rise apartment blocks, squeezing every penny out of the available land. Exactly what his father hadn't wanted to happen when he'd entrusted the family estate to him. The actions of the ne'er-do-well son he'd purported not to be.

Ewen was glad he'd come to his senses. Happy that Bonnie had crashed into his life and given him some happy memories here, and the promise of making a lot more together.

He looked at the glossy photographs, essentially a sales catalogue of his family home, and felt nothing but revulsion that he'd even considered the idea of flogging his heritage to the highest bidder. It was the only link he had left to his family, and though at one time he would've been thankful to be rid of even that, the letter from his father had healed some of those old wounds.

He looked at the photographs of his father's study where they were currently sitting, of the desk where he and Bonnie had finally taken a chance on their feelings for one another, and was certain of his next move.

'The castle is not for sale. I'm sorry for wasting your time, and I'll pay for all the work you've done thus far, but I've changed my mind.' Ewen tossed the brochure back across the desk.

Mr Argyle blinked at him, temporarily stunned into silence. Ewen surmised he probably wasn't used to being told no, and watched as the stunned expression turned to something darker.

'I'm aware you weren't ready to sell just yet. Apologies if I've jumped the gun. I'm sure you just need some time to think things through properly.'

Ewen got to his feet, deciding the meeting was over. 'Sorry. I'm not going to change my mind. I'm staying on at the castle for good. It's my home.'

He shook hands with Mr Argyle, who clearly wasn't going to give up without a fight. 'I'll leave the brochure with you anyway, and you have my number if things don't work out the way you plan.'

Ignoring Ewen's protest, he removed the paperwork from the binder and left it on the desk. Ewen saw him to the door, confident their paths would never cross again.

'Is everything okay?' Mrs McKenzie walked up beside him, hands fidgeting with the buttons on her cardigan as she watched Mr Argyle get into his flashy sports car.

Ewen didn't know how much information his visitor had shared with her, but it was clear she was anxious.

'Yes. I was on the verge of doing something stupid, but I came to my senses.'

Mrs McKenzie's worried frown smoothed out into a smile. 'Bonnie's been good for you.'

His housekeeper's astuteness still had the ability to surprise him. 'How did you…? I thought you didn't approve.'

Mrs McKenzie patted him on the arm. 'It's not that I didn't approve, Ewen. I was concerned. I didn't want you to make any rash decisions that might jeopardise your future here. But I can tell she's helped you make the right ones.'

She gave him a squeeze before walking away, leaving him staring after her in disbelief.

'I'm just heading out to see my solicitor. I'll be back later,' he called out, grabbing his coat on his way out of the door.

He didn't want to lose her or Bonnie, the two most important women in his life, and he was going to take steps to make sure of that.

Ewen was conspicuous by his absence and Bonnie hadn't been able to settle in the shop, worried he'd had second thoughts again. After all, it was a big jump from a supposed casual fling into an actual relationship, and he'd been antsy first time around.

'Thank you. Have a good day.' She handed over another paper bag full of her chocolates and watched her last customer disappear out of the door.

Business had been steady this morning, but it appeared to have died down again, so she made the call to take a quick break. She turned the closed sign on the door, locked the shop, and decided to go looking for Ewen. If they needed to have 'the talk' she would rather do it soon than spend the rest of the day wondering and worrying.

Bonnie ventured downstairs, among the new crop of visitors making their way into the castle. Ewen often liked to mingle with the guests and provide a more personal touch to their tours.

'Are you taking an early lunch?' Mrs McKenzie, with her ninja-like stealth, appeared in the sitting-room area beside her without making a sound.

'Something like that. I was looking for Ewen… the duke. I know he said he had an appointment, but I thought he would've been finished by now.' She'd be lying if she said she wasn't curious about the nature of his meeting, but not everything that happened at the castle was her business.

It was early days in their relationship. So early she was already doubting if they had one. It would probably take a while before he thought to include her in any decision-making, if ever. Though Bonnie would like to feel a part of it all if they were looking towards a future together. Especially when this was her home and livelihood too.

'Yes, he had a meeting in the study earlier, but I think he said something about going out to see his solicitor.'

'Okay, thanks. I'll catch up with him later.'

Before Bonnie could leave the group currently marvelling at the huge fireplace, and paintings of men on horseback that covered the walls from floor to ceiling, Mrs McKenzie caught her arm.

'He's thinking about the future of the castle, but he also needs to do what's right for him.'

Bonnie nodded in agreement, even though she didn't know what the woman was referring to. Mrs McKenzie and Ewen were close and he'd obviously confided in her about whatever he was up to today. Whilst Bonnie was glad he had someone to look out for him, who'd known him his entire life, it irked that he hadn't been able to confide in her. Especially after what they'd shared, and when they'd planned to be in a committed relationship. Now she wasn't sure of anything.

She made her way to the study and knocked on the door.

'Ewen?' When there was no reply, she took a peek inside in case he'd fallen asleep after his nocturnal exertions last night.

There was no sign of him, but he'd left the windows open, causing a breeze to chill the room. When she went to close them, she noticed some papers on the floor that must have blown off the desk.

She hadn't meant to look, and she was sorry

she did in the end. It was a sales brochure for the castle. As her heart broke into a million shards, she flicked through the pages of glossy pictures offering her home as an amazing property investment. Not an important, historic site, or a castle that had been on the land for generations of the Harris family. Or her home, the place she'd imagined a future with Ewen.

Worse than the idea of the place being sold, possibly to a property developer who'd likely swamp every inch of surrounding land with new houses, was the fact that Ewen had been keeping this from her. Once again, she'd been lied to, conned into a relationship by someone who'd purported to want the best for her. He'd let her get comfortable, let her defences down again, believing she'd found someone she could trust, in a place she'd come to call home. Then spectacularly broken her trust.

She knew then it was over.

Tears clouding her vision, she ran to her room and immediately started to pack her case. She had a few more clothes than she'd first arrived with, but she managed to squeeze everything in. Minus the red dress, which was hanging up in her wardrobe, because she knew she couldn't look at it without thinking of the ball at the castle, and Ewen. All of which she'd lost with the discovery of his betrayal.

She didn't understand why he was doing it. The castle was his home, his business, the last link to his family, and it wasn't as though he were short of money. Mrs McKenzie had talked about him making the right decision for his future, and perhaps that meant moving on somewhere else.

'Well, good for you!' she shouted into the empty wardrobe. This new life he was setting up clearly didn't involve her, when he was making plans to sell her home from under her without as much as a discussion.

Bonnie heaved her case off the bed, grabbed her jacket and handbag and made her way downstairs.

'Bonnie? Where are you off to?' Mrs McKenzie met her on the staircase.

She had hoped to get out of here unseen, with a short note to tell Ewen she'd gone. It was clear the housekeeper wanted more information, but she didn't have any to give.

'Honestly? I don't know, but I can't stay here any more with someone I can't trust.' Ewen had fooled her into thinking he was different, that he wouldn't hurt her. With that false sense of security, she'd given him her heart, taking a leap of faith that he wouldn't break it. Only to find he'd betrayed her already. Manipulating her, taking advantage of her feelings for him, was everything she'd been afraid of happening.

She should never have let her guard down so easily when he'd toyed with her feelings once already. Only a fool would have given him a chance to do it again. She certainly wasn't going to stick around and find out what else he was capable of.

With her eyes on the front door, she continued her escape, unwilling to be delayed in case she did run into Ewen and couldn't control her emotions. Whether they would manifest in tears or anger she couldn't predict and would rather not wait to find out.

Mrs McKenzie hurried down the stairs after her. 'Please, Bonnie, wait and talk to Ewen. He at least deserves that.'

Bonnie hesitated at the open door. 'I don't owe him anything.'

If her last relationship had taught her anything it was that she wasn't beholden to anyone. She wasn't going to let another man manipulate her emotions, using guilt and charm to keep her in a toxic relationship. The fact that he was already hiding the truth from her so early on set off so many alarms, and this time she was going to listen to them.

With a final act of defiance, she slammed the front door shut, and closed another painful chapter of her life. Whilst she'd had some good times within the castle walls, and a business she was proud of, she loved herself more, and needed to leave for her own sanity.

The wheels of her case clattered over the cobbles as she made her way down the tree-lined lane towards the main road. It was only then she realised she didn't know where she was going.

There was one place she'd contemplated returning to one day, and right now she was out of options. If that didn't work out, she'd have to start over somewhere else. She'd proved she could live independently, manage her own workplace, and survive the toughest of circumstances. Though she didn't relish the prospect of moving to a new town, setting up again, she knew she was capable of doing it. She didn't need anyone, but she also knew how comforting it was to have someone who felt like home.

Bonnie took out her phone and dialled her parents' number, hoping they hadn't changed it in the intervening years. Her heart was in her throat as she listened to the dial tone, waiting to speak to people who might not forgive her behaviour and could very well add to her pain. But she was willing to take the chance and admit she'd been wrong if it meant healing their broken relationship. Her parents had had her best interests at heart, it had simply taken her a long time to recognise that. They'd loved her once, and she hoped, if she explained everything she'd been through, they could find it in their hearts to do so again when she needed them most.

'Hello?' The voice answering the phone almost broke her and she had to swallow down the sudden welling of emotion. All she wanted to do was throw herself into her mother's arms and cry out her heartbreak, but she knew there was a long way to go until then.

'Mum?'

'Bonnie, is that you?' When the sound of her mother promptly bursting into tears quickly followed, Bonnie knew she at least had somewhere to go.

'You sit there, Dad. I'll go and make you a cup of tea.' Bonnie helped her father into an armchair, waiting patiently as he huffed and puffed his way into a comfortable position.

'What about the shop?'

'The shop's closed, Dad. Remember?' It had broken her heart to come back and find the place boarded up. Worse still, to discover how badly her father's health had deteriorated during their years of estrangement. He seemed to have aged rapidly, skin and bone compared to the robust, imposing figure she remembered from her youth. Her mother too now looked old beyond her years, caring for her ailing husband clearly taking its toll.

'Oh, yes. I got too old for it and you weren't here to take over the way I always hoped you would.'

The guilt pierced her very soul at the mess she'd left behind. Perhaps if she'd come back sooner she could've salvaged the shop, maybe even something of her parents' health. Now she counted herself lucky she at least got to see them, and hadn't ended up like Ewen, full of regret and remorse.

'Well, she's back now and that's all that matters.' Her mother bustled in with the tea already made, fixing the tray on her father's lap, and giving Bonnie a grateful smile.

All the animosity between them had dissipated the minute they'd been reunited, her parents so tearfully happy to see her again.

'I'm going to have a look later and see if I can get some part-time shop work so I can contribute. It would give me time here too to help you with things around the house.' The family home, which had once been spotless, was now cluttered, laundry and dirty dishes dotted around, her mother clearly struggling to cope with everything.

It wasn't the life she'd planned for herself, but for whatever time left her parents had, she wanted them to be comfortable. They were her family after all.

'I'm so glad you're home. We thought we'd never see you again.' It was the umpteenth time her mother had uttered the same sentiment over the past week, always teary when she did.

Bonnie hadn't left any contact details when she'd had her rebellion, running off with Ed, the worst thing to happen to her. Then fear and manipulation had prevented her from getting in touch and admitting her parents had been right all along. After cutting her off from anyone who'd loved her, Ed had convinced her no one would want her back. That she wasn't worthy of love and they'd been glad to be rid of her.

She could see now by isolating her in such a manner it had made it easier for him to control her. Making her believe he was the only person in her life who cared about her, despite the opposite being true.

According to her mother, her father had become very introspective after their only child left, parting on less than favourable terms. They'd missed her, regretted any harsh words spoken in the heat of the moment, but hadn't been able to make amends because they'd had no idea where she'd gone.

Even though it had been difficult for everyone, she'd been honest about what had happened between her and Ed. She hadn't thought it necessary to tell them all the gruesome details, but enough for them to understand why she hadn't been in contact. There had been tears and apologies on both sides, and she'd felt a huge weight lifted off her shoulders as she'd opened up. As if she'd finally left the past behind her.

The past seven days had been spent trying to make a dent in the housework, and helping take care of her dad. It was at night in bed her thoughts turned to Ewen and the life she'd thought she had at the castle. That was a loss she didn't think she'd ever get over, but she hadn't had a choice but to leave it all behind.

She didn't want to spend another decade trapped in a relationship with another man who thought he could play games with her heart, and who obviously didn't respect her. Why else would he have made plans to sell the castle without telling her? Perhaps he hoped she'd simply go along with whatever he decided, or, worse, would drop her once someone more suitable came on the scene. He was ambitious, where she just wanted somewhere she felt safe and secure. Ewen had ruined all of that.

At least coming back here, helping her parents, was a decision she'd made herself. It wasn't something that had been imposed upon her.

'You sit down too, Mum. I can sort out the washing.' She didn't want her mother's health impacted too, and was doing her best to lighten the load. At least when Bonnie was busy with laundry, or washing dishes, she didn't have time to dwell on her broken heart.

Once she got her mother seated, her feet up, with a cup of tea, Bonnie set to work in the kitchen. In the middle of her loading the washing machine the doorbell rang at the front of the house.

'Typical,' she muttered to herself. 'I'll get it, Mum. Don't get up.'

She deposited the wash basket with the rest of the dirty clothes onto the kitchen worktop to resume once she saw off whatever visitor was at the door. In a fit of pique, she yanked the front door open.

'Yes? What do you want?' The frustrated words died on her lips when she saw who it was standing on the step.

'Ewen?'

'That pleasant tone brings back so many memories...' He grinned, making her confused about whether she wanted to hit him or hug him for showing up here unannounced and breaking her heart all over again.

'What do you want?' she repeated, arms folded, chin tilted up into the air, denying him the knowledge that she cared.

'You.'

The fluttering in her stomach went ignored,

because she clearly couldn't trust her instincts around handsome men.

'Too bad.' She went to slam the door in his face to show him she remained out of reach, but he stuck a foot in the way, and stepped inside instead.

They were toe to toe in the cramped hallway and she took a step back to regain some personal space and a clear head.

'Do you know how hard it was to find you?'

'No, and I don't care.' Bonnie tried to convince herself it didn't matter why he'd felt the need to follow her. He was probably miffed because she hadn't fallen into line, that she'd decided what happened in her future instead of him.

'We both know that's not true, but I'll tell you anyway. Since you neglected to answer any of my calls or messages, I had to do a bit of detective work. I remembered you telling me your father had a chocolate shop, so I did a bit of digging and found an old listing for this address.' He looked so pleased with himself she couldn't wait to wipe the smile off his face.

Coming here was supposed to mark the end of her time with Ewen, the beginning of her new relationship with her parents. Now he was blurring those two definitive lines in the sand that she'd made, with his big stompy boots.

'Doesn't sound *that* hard. You've found me. Whoop-de-whoop. It wasn't a treasure hunt, X doesn't mark the spot, and you don't get a prize.' Unfortunately, she didn't find the satisfaction she'd hoped for in watching his face fall.

'You are the prize, Bonnie. You always were.'

'Yeah? I felt more of a convenience.' The pain and anger she'd been bottling up since that afternoon came bubbling to the surface now she finally had an outlet for it.

'That's not true. I wanted to come after you sooner, but I thought you'd decided you didn't want to be in a relationship with me after all. I knew it had to be serious when you left the chocolate shop behind. That's why I gave you some space. I just didn't want you to think I didn't respect your decision.'

'Yet here you are…'

'I missed you. You have no idea how much. The castle hasn't been the same without you. I can't even bear to open the shop. Life is so lonely now you're not part of it, and I just need to know why. All you said in the note was that you weren't prepared to let another man dictate your life. Whatever I did, or didn't do, I'm sorry. Mrs McKenzie was in a terrible state after you left too. I think she was as heartbroken to see you go as I was.' He scrubbed his hands over his scalp and she could see his obvious distress, her defences gradually crumbling with every utterance of remorse.

'I would've thought it made things easier for you. I'm sure it's more difficult to sell a property with a sitting tenant.'

Ewen's forehead knitted into a frown. 'What are you talking about?'

Bonnie let out an exaggerated sigh. 'Don't pretend you don't know. At least do me the courtesy of being honest. It doesn't matter now when I've no intention of going back.'

Gaslighting her into thinking it was all in her head didn't work on her any more. She'd since learned it was a preferred tool of the controlling male.

When he continued to stare at her with that puzzled expression, she lost the last of her patience.

'You were selling the castle, my home, and my business from under me. Apparently, I wasn't even worthy of a discussion over my future.'

Ewen let out a long breath. 'I'm not selling the castle.'

'I saw the brochure. Mrs McKenzie said you were making some big decisions on your future. It didn't take much working out.'

'It might have looked that way. I suppose I haven't been upfront about everything at the castle.'

Bonnie *tsked* at the eventual confession, knowing she'd been right all along. Now he was going to try and worm his way out of it, the way her ex always had.

'Part of my father's will stipulated that I had to stay at the castle for a year before I could sell it on. When I first arrived, I was grieving for him, angry at myself and my parents. Mostly at him for forcing me to stay somewhere that held such painful memories. So I had made enquiries about selling up when the time came. That was before you came into my life, Bonnie. Before everything changed.'

Her heart began to pitter patter, the sliver of hope that she hadn't lost him for ever, that he wasn't like her ex after all, shining brightly. 'You had a meeting that morning, presumably with the estate agent, and Mrs McKenzie said you'd gone to see your solicitor. What was I supposed to think?'

'That I love you and was making plans for our future.' He took her trembling hands in his. She was barely holding onto the last of her defences.

'I had a long-standing appointment with the estate agent I forgot to cancel. He'd taken it upon himself to make a mock-up property brochure. I told him I'd changed my mind. That I was staying on.'

'And the solicitor?' Slowly, the reasons she'd

thought she'd had to leave were being shot to pieces, and she was clinging onto the theory he hadn't had her interests at heart before she completely capitulated.

It was the first time he'd said he loved her. Words that had been used in the past to control and coerce her, and she was afraid to believe now. Once she trusted in his feelings, she would have to be open with her own, and that left her vulnerable to more hurt.

Ewen's smile tried to convince her everything was okay, that she'd worried for nothing, but she'd been burned one too many times to let that sway her.

'I did go to discuss business at the castle, and my future in a way. I had a contract drawn up to sign over the chocolate shop to you. It's your business now, and I had hoped it would help you feel more secure at the castle.'

He pulled a wad of papers from inside his wax jacket and handed them over to her. 'The offer's still there. Even if you don't want to give me another chance, you have a place at the castle.'

It was a commitment she'd never expected, and, though she wanted to jump at the chance, her circumstances had changed.

'I can't leave my parents. Dad isn't well, and Mum is struggling to care for him. They had to close the shop. I can't just walk away again.' Her conscience wouldn't let her, even if her heart was elsewhere.

'In case you didn't hear me, Bonnie, I love you. I'll do whatever it takes to keep you in my life. Your parents can come too. There's plenty of space, and we can get them whatever help they need. I promise you, I was making plans for our future together. In hindsight, yes, I should've consulted you first, but I think I've learned my lesson. Do you think you can forgive me?' He slipped his hands around her waist and pulled her closer, and Bonnie knew she already had.

'I do have some stipulations,' she said, not wanting to appear too easily won over. There needed to be a precedent set for the future.

'Of course.'

'I want to move into your apartment.'

'Naturally. If we're living together, I want us to be together, not sleeping in separate rooms.'

'I'll expect you to run me a bath at least once a week. Dinner together every night.'

'As long as that includes the odd takeaway.'

Bonnie nodded. 'And a promise to continue with the annual ball.'

'I think that's a definite anyway, or I'll never hear the end of it from Mrs McKenzie. How about the promise of the first dance?'

'Done.' Bonnie held her hand out to shake Ewen's hand, but once the handshake had sealed the deal, he pulled her closer, and took her in his arms.

'Please don't leave me again.' His kiss, so full of love and desire, made her wonder why she ever had.

Now that he'd made that commitment, assured her of his feelings, Bonnie was able to finally speak hers aloud without fear.

'I won't. I love you too much.' She hugged him tight, never wanting to let go.

Bonnie had finally found the unconditional love she'd been looking for her entire life, and she knew her future was safe in Ewen's hands. He was invested in their relationship, and their life at the castle, as much as she was.

EPILOGUE

'CAN I STEAL you away for lunch?' Ewen appeared in the shop once all the customers had gone.

Bonnie ruefully glanced at the now empty shelves in the display case. 'I can't. We had a run on the whisky truffles.'

They'd become a firm favourite in the shop, probably due to the duke's favourable reviews, which he liked to share with the visitors before they stopped by.

'You go. I can restock with the ones you made earlier.' Her mum gave her a nudge, not that it took much to convince Bonnie to take time out to be with Ewen.

It had been five months since she'd reunited with her parents. Four months since they'd sold up the house and shop to move into the castle with them. Since then, they'd all been finding a new way of life. Her mother's workload had considerably lessened now there were cleaners on hand to take care of the communal rooms, and they'd even got some home help to assist with her father's day-to-day care.

With Bonnie's chocolate shop beginning to flourish, she'd needed an extra hand to help meet demand. When her mother had expressed an interest in working a few hours, it had seemed like the perfect fit. After all, she'd had experience working in the family shop too. Meeting new people and finding an interest of her own had reinvigorated her mother, and Bonnie was glad to see her enjoying life.

'If you're sure?' She was already taking off her apron and heading towards Ewen. Even though they were living together in his apartment, she never liked to miss an opportunity to be with him. It was safe to say they were loved up.

'I thought we could eat in,' he said cryptically, leading her to the study.

'What on earth...?' The desk had been covered with a red and white gingham cloth and was laid out with plates of delicious food.

Bonnie wandered over to take a closer look, spotting the bottle of champagne cooling in the ice bucket, the bowl of scrumptious-looking strawberries, the dainty finger sandwiches and home-baked scones. Her mouth was watering already.

'Did you do all of this?' She helped herself to one of the fresh strawberries and took a bite.

'I had some help…'

Mrs McKenzie, she presumed. The woman had been so much more than a member of staff to both of them, helping Bonnie's parents settle into their new surroundings. As well as helping her mother take care of her father, she often escorted him to the chocolate shop to enjoy a cup of tea and a sweet treat whilst he watched her mother work. With his heart problems and his early-stage dementia, there was no way of knowing how long they'd have him here, but Bonnie wanted to make sure he was happy and comfortable for whatever time he had left. Certainly, this was the most relaxed she'd ever seen her parents.

'Well, it's all appreciated. I'm starving.' She didn't take gestures like this for granted and it felt to her that Ewen went out of his way every day to make sure she knew she was loved. Something she would never tire of, and took comfort from on a daily basis.

He poured two flutes full of champagne, but before he handed one to her, he turned and took her hands in his.

'I can't tell you how much these past months have meant to me, Bonnie. Having you all here has made me feel like part of a family again.'

She didn't know what had brought on this outpouring of sentiment, but it was further confirmation that the arrangement was working well for all parties. A commitment many men would've shied away from, especially so early on in their relationship. But Ewen had bent over backwards to accommodate her parents, giving them rooms large enough for whatever possessions they wanted to bring with them. If she was honest, she'd expected some resistance from her mother and father to being uprooted and transported into the middle of a local tourist attraction, but they'd been on board from the start. It had taken a weight off their shoulders and given them all an opportunity to build some bridges. All thanks to Ewen.

'None of it would've been possible if you hadn't been so accommodating. Thank you.' She tilted her face up to kiss him full on the lips, expressing her love for him the best way she knew how.

'Marry me.'

'What?'

'It's not quite how I'd imagined this going, but I'm in the moment. Go with it.'

Bonnie opened and closed her mouth, speechless. Suddenly it all made sense, the romantic lunch date, the champagne, and a very eager Ewen.

'Ask me again.' She wanted to know she hadn't imagined it or misheard him.

Ewen disentangled himself from her and got

down on one knee, leaving her in no doubt about his intentions. 'Bonnie Abernathy, will you do me the honour of becoming my wife and the new lady of the castle?'

There was only one title that mattered to her, and that was becoming Mrs Harris. She was simply very fortunate she got to call this place home too.

'Yes. A million times yes. I love you, Ewen, and I want to be with you for ever.'

He gathered her up in a hug and swung her around, his joy as palpable as her own.

Bonnie's future was bright. It was with Ewen, and she couldn't think of a better man to spend the rest of her life with.

* * * * *

*If you enjoyed this story,
check out these other great reads
from Karin Baine*

An American Doctor in Ireland
Surgeon Prince's Fake Fiancée
A Mother for His Little Princess
Nurse's Risk with the Rebel

All available now!